the Red One

Safia Fazlul

MAWENZI
HOUSE

We acknowledge the support of the Canada Council for the Arts for our publishing program. We also acknowledge support from the Government of Ontario through the Ontario Arts Council, and the support of the Government of Canada through the Canada Book Fund.

Cover design by Peggy Stockdale
Cover image: virtu studio / Tea cup on pastel pink background. Top view / Shutterstock

Library and Archives Canada Cataloguing in Publication

Title: The Red One / Safia Fazlul.
Names: Fazlul, Safia, author.
Identifiers: Canadiana (print) 20230548555 | Canadiana (ebook) 20230548563 | ISBN 9781774151150 (softcover) | ISBN 9781774151167 (EPUB) | ISBN 9781774151174 (PDF)
Subjects: LCGFT: Novels.
Classification: LCC PS8611.A98 R43 2023 | DDC C813/.6—dc23

Printed and bound in Canada by Coach House Printing

Mawenzi House Publishers Ltd.
39 Woburn Avenue (B)
Toronto, Ontario M5M 1K5
Canada

www.mawenzihouse.com

1

I WAS TWELVE YEARS old when I first met evil.

As always, my father was at work and my mother, fed up with me and my brother, Tariq, had as usual chosen to ignore us. It was a Saturday, that unforgettable day, the first weekend after the last day of school before summer break. My mother knew she was stuck with us every single day until September. Her mood was always colder in the summer.

My father drove a cab from sunrise to sunset and my mother was a beautiful housewife. We lived in a three-bedroom apartment in a rundown corner of Toronto which housed many other immigrants from South Asia. My parents, Muslim Indians loyal to the traditions of the old country and obsessively religious, had a stellar reputation in the community. They valued their reputation more than they valued money because the latter they didn't have and the former secured invitations to parties, networking, and a sort of social validation they could not get anywhere else.

"Can you take me to the park please, Ma?" Tariq pleaded over breakfast. "My friends are all going there today."

Seven-year-old Tariq had a bad habit of talking while eating.

As a result his food often slid down his cleft chin and dirtied up the tablecloth, leaving my mother infuriated. She could not bear to see dirt in her house.

"Chew with your mouth closed!" she yelled from the kitchen in Hindi, ignoring Tariq's question, which she probably hadn't heard properly.

She had spent all morning tending to the potted flowers in the balcony and was now washing the dirt off her hands in the sink. Her makeshift garden in our pigeon-poop-covered balcony was one of her main distractions from a monotonous life divided between cooking, cleaning, and fighting with my father.

My mother loved us quietly. She was adequate. She couldn't speak English and thus being unemployable, she was stuck indoors playing the traditional housewife in a loveless arranged marriage. She always made sure Tariq and I got all our meals, our clothes were always clean, and we had all the necessary school supplies. Maybe that was the reason she never allowed us to complain.

We were never to discuss our feelings, our dreams, and especially our worries. She had a unique way of dismissing those conversations and twisting them into something about Islam and God. We spent more time discussing the unseen and the unknown than each other. She made a strong effort never to reveal too much about herself and never to discover too much about us. She wouldn't let us make her feel old.

My mother handed Tariq a napkin before joining us at the dining table with a cup of tea. She always sat across from us, her chair a little pulled away, gazing at her beloved balcony.

"So, can you take me, Ma? Pleeeease?" Tariq wiped his mouth clumsily.

My mother held her cup of tea delicately with her slim fingers as I watched her with quiet admiration. She was always beautiful to look at: a svelte woman with porcelain skin glowing against her waist-long, glossy black hair. She had large hazel eyes, alert but innocent as a doe's, and a wide smile that always reached them. If you didn't know her, she could've easily been mistaken for someone warm and welcoming.

"Pleeeease?" Tariq pleaded.

My little brother was overweight and short for his age, sporting thick-framed glasses under greasy black hair. He hated reading, had no interest in religion, and would spend all day in front of the TV or the computer. He was the one my parents worried about; I was the brilliant, fair-skinned, and pious golden child. My parents never told me they were proud of me, but they told everybody else. They would brag about me to anybody who would listen about all the great things I would surely achieve.

I was thin and pretty, and although popular and friendly, I spent hour upon hour reading my Islamic books alone in my room. I wanted to know everything about Islam. I wanted to be the greatest twelve-year-old Muslim in the neighbourhood and in our community. My intention was not to enter heaven; I just wanted my parents to notice me.

"Ma? Are you listening to me?" Tariq began stomping his feet.

I noticed the annoyed look on her face and kicked Tariq's leg under the table, mouthing "Be quiet!"

I was expected to control Tariq. According to my mother, it was my natural duty to help her raise him because not only was I the firstborn, I was also a girl. Good daughters happily do the work of their mothers.

"We're not going to the park today because we have other plans," my mother announced. "Your Aunty Khan has invited us over for lunch."

"Yes!" Tariq cheered, nearly spitting out his breakfast in delight, "Aunty Khan is the best!"

Tariq loved going to the Khans because he was guaranteed a table full of cakes and a gift bag full of brand-new toys.

The Khans were a wealthy and well-connected Aunty and Uncle often seen at community events. They were big donors. They had met my parents at an Islamic conference years ago and hit it off with them. My parents, moneyless devotees of God who could recite the Quran from memory, were an exotic addition to the Khans' circle of rich immigrants. I understand now that piety—just like everything else—was a show in the Khans' world, there being an implicit competition on who could show more of it. The rich immigrants wanted the biggest house, the nicest car, the kid with the most degrees, and to offset and conceal this blatant, un-Islamic greed, they also wanted to be the loudest Muslims.

"Do I have to go?" I moaned pointlessly to my mother.

No matter how many delicious desserts they served, I was never fond of the Khans. Even at just twelve, I could see beyond all their glitter and gifts. They were performers, and we were a hungry, indiscriminate audience. My parents were easily impressed by Uncle Khan's exaggerated stories about his travels, Auntie Khan's endless display of gold jewellery, and the many gifts they so casually threw at Tariq and me. But they were not charitable, they were patronizing. They wanted us around to show off how much better their lives were. They liked us because they were not like us.

"Of course you must go," my mother said in her language, "you have no reason not to."

"I don't really like them."

"Nisha," she added sternly, "they may have more than us, but they are good people. No need to be jealous of them."

"Yeah, Nisha, don't be jealous!" Tariq chimed in. "Jealousy is a sin."

My mother nodded approvingly.

It was not worth arguing. I wasn't jealous of the Khans. Although we were not rich, I had never felt deprived. I envied the Khans' freedom with time. Unlike my father, Uncle Khan was some important businessman who could set his own hours and be home whenever he wanted.

To my mother the Khans were special. She was impressed by their success and lifestyles; they had realized the dream of South Asian immigrants—her own people with roots in a village like hers where poverty was abundant, and hope was scarce. In her eyes, the Khans were angels. They could do no wrong because they were blessed beings sent down to give everybody else hope.

Poverty had stolen my father away from me. He worked seven days a week, starting from before Tariq and I had woken up to late evening just after dinner. I used to watch my dad at the kitchen table, eating his rice ravenously after a long day of driving people around in his cab. My mother always said not to disturb him while he was eating. I tried to talk to him when he was finished, but after a short while of feigning interest in my childish stories he always dozed off on the couch. We barely spoke because we barely saw each other awake.

My parents often squabbled. My mother resented that she was always stuck at home doing all the housework and childcare. He would shoot down her complaints with a simple reminder that it was his money that paid for her Canadian lifestyle, modest though it might be by other standards. If it wasn't for him bringing her to Canada, she'd still be inhaling the smog with the sunburnt beggars back home.

They hated each other. Money wouldn't have fixed that, but

it could have given us all more space. I'm sure the Khans could just walk away to the opposite ends of their mansion to cool off during an argument; their kids could hide in their rooms upstairs. Admittedly, I was jealous of this.

"I'm not jealous," I argued with my mother. "I just don't like being around them."

She put up her hand in a stop sign to show that she was done listening to me and declared, "They are good people with lots of good connections. One day, they can help me find a quality husband for you."

I blushed, and Tariq giggled.

"I don't care if you're jealous of them or if you just don't like high-class people, we are going there today, and you will show your Aunty Khan the utmost respect. Now go shower and wear something clean and colourful."

Aunty and Uncle Khan may indeed have been angels, but they had a demon living in their house. This demon was the real reason I wanted to stay far away from them. She was their exceptionally beautiful but cruel daughter. Her name was Sonia.

Sonia always reminded me of my place. Just her presence alone, spectacular and indestructible like a polished marble statue overlooking the rest of us mortals, held up a mirror to all my imperfections and shortcomings. She had an enviable confidence; she spoke whatever thoughts were floating in her mind because she knew nobody would dare challenge her. Especially not I.

The long drive to the Khans' house always instilled a terrible fear in me. The further we drove away from the busy traffic of the inner city, the more I squirmed in my seat. Just like in a horror movie, you'd have to drive through empty winding roads with nothing but trees for miles to get to their street. The houses there lay behind tall hedges and elaborate gates as if they all had something to hide.

"Both of you better behave," my mother said as she applied her red lipstick in the rear-view mirror. "Don't embarrass me." Her silky black hair she'd neatly tied into a bun at the nape of her neck. She didn't conceal her hair with a hijab, but she would also never leave it loose to flow sexily in public. Wearing the hijab wasn't common traditionally where she came from and so she never pushed me to wear it. I knew from all my studying of Islam that I was supposed to cover my hair for the sake of modesty, but it was never the religion I passionately followed—it was my mother who followed it.

The closer we arrived at the Khans' home the more my mother's shoulders hunched with shame. Our old, scratched and dented sedan went along like a dirty old beggar on the wealthy, gated mansions. The Khans had left their gate open for us and we turned into their cobblestone driveway. My mother sighed with longing.

"Woah!" Tariq gasped as we arrived, stunned by the three-floor house in the distance although he had seen it before.

"Don't act so impressed," my mother exclaimed. "They will think we are below them."

We were not below them, but we surely didn't belong here. No matter how polite and classy we behaved, we had nothing in common with the Khans except ethnicity and religion. Nostalgia about her youth in a communal village thousands of miles away was enough for my naïve mother to befriend and trust people.

In fact, the Khans' house stood out from their neighbours'. They may have lived amongst seasoned, progressive white Canadians, but they very much belonged to us, the South

Asian immigrant community. Their neighbours had renovated and modernized their houses into sleek and soulless squares, but the Khans had done nothing to fiddle with their house's old and romantic charm.

I remember the lilies. Endless rows of white lilies hugging every curve of the Khans' driveway like dandruff along a hairline. There were other flowers too, some purple and many pink, but I remember the white lilies because they were present from the gate all the way to the garage and around the house. We parked our car and followed a red brick pathway to the main door where the lilies would follow along, scent and all.

"One day, inshallah, we will have a garden with this many plants." My mother stopped briefly to admire the swaying white blossoms.

I was secretly wishing that day would never come. She was already far too busy with her potted flowers in the balcony; if she had a whole garden to tend to, she'd never talk to me again.

A beaming Aunty Khan welcomed us. She was dressed in a silk canary salwaar kameez that exaggerated her large hips and breasts. She was a chunky woman with a plain face and hennaed hair peeking through a loosely wrapped hijab. If it weren't for her oversized gold jewellery and bright red lipstick, her appearance would be rather subdued. She was probably aware of this fact and made up for it in spades with her deafening personality.

"Hello, my lovely kids!" Aunty Khan tussled Tariq's thick bangs before she threw her hefty, bearish arms around me. "I ordered so much food for you!"

"Salam Alaikum. Thank you for inviting us, Aunty," Tariq and I mumbled the rehearsed greeting.

My face sank into Aunty Khan's soft chest and I took in the enchanting scent of expensive perfume and minty body wash. When my mother hugged me, there was always the distinct smell of vegetable oil and spices. My mother's hugs were always brief and finished with two quick pats on my back as if to silently console me for having to go back to her cooking and not giving me enough affection.

Aunty Khan and my mother kissed each other on the cheeks before my mother began the usual and expected list of compliments. *Your house looks amazing. You look amazing. Those earrings are stunning. I love your outfit.*

"Oh, stop it," Aunty Khan waved her hand dismissively. "The kids look hungry, let's feed them!"

Tariq's eyes lit up at the mention of food and he skipped into the house along with my mother. I followed slackly behind with Aunty Khan's heavy hand around my bony shoulder.

"You're becoming a beautiful young lady, Nisha," Aunty Khan sized me up from top to bottom, "definitely taking after your mother, mashallah."

I recoiled with embarrassment over my recently enlarging hips and breasts. My cheeks reddened as I looked to my mother, clueless as to what to say. My mother said to never make a big deal about compliments because it didn't matter how attractive I was. Beauty was to be hidden from all the eyes of the world except my future husband's. Only sinful, vain, shameless women showed off their beauty for all to see.

She chuckled, "If Nisha is so beautiful, why don't you introduce her to Riad?"

"Oh, I don't think your daughter could handle me as her mother-in-law!" Aunty Khan retorted jokingly, and the two women buckled with laughter.

Riad was the Khans' oldest child and only son. I had seen him only once on an Eid day, when I was nine years old. He was even more reclusive and repelled by guests than his sister. An acne-faced teenager had driven up to the front door in a very fancy convertible. He wore flashy brand-name clothes and his hair, rigidly gelled upward, resembled the comb of a proud rooster, as I imagined it. He came inside and Uncle Khan commanded him to greet us. He mumbled "salaam" to my parents, nodded with slight acknowledgement at Tariq and me, and went upstairs to his room. Soon he came down and drove off.

"I have to get that boy married before he brings home a Canadian girl," Aunty Khan laughed and gestured for us to leave the marble-floored foyer. "All these university kids have a boyfriend or girlfriend."

We strolled along behind a nonstop chatting Aunty Khan as we glanced up at the ceiling. It was impressively tall and always drew attention. I always felt like an undersized alien when visiting here, no matter how kindly Aunty Khan treated us.

An arched doorway framed by a carved quotation from the Quran welcomed us to the dining room. Written in gold text over a green cloth, it was probably the only thing in the house that didn't fit a beige, white, and light blue theme. I wondered if the Khans genuinely believed whatever it said.

"These haram relationships are ruining our youth," my mother started. "They don't focus on their studies, only dreaming about boyfriends and girlfriends. They're committing sin and moving further away from religion. They don't know love is only temporary. God is forever."

Beneath a dazzling chandelier stood the extended, polished dining table overflowing with all kinds of food. Tariq and I eyed the delicacies our parents could afford to feed us only occasionally: lamb chops, beef ribs, chicken wings, kebabs, and platefuls of colourful pastries—a far cry from our normal dal, vegetable, and rice.

Tariq and I didn't hesitate to pick up our forks and knives.

Not even the incessant conversation between our mother and Aunty Khan could stop us from stuffing our mouths. Their conversations always centred around the same essential topic: marriage. Who got married? Who's getting married? Who should get married? Even back then, at the naive age of twelve, I found it ironic that two women who spent most of the day alone in a kitchen were obsessed with speculating about the union of two other people.

"Finding a good girl for Riad is no easy task though." Aunty Khan looked defeated as she filled her plate. "There are dozens of proposals from very good families back home but Riad wants a girl from here."

My mom shook her head with disapproval and scoffed, "The girls here don't pray. I must remind Nisha all the time of prayers. Her nose is always stuck in some book about science."

I couldn't defend myself with my mouth stuffed, so I just smiled coyly at Aunty Khan, trying to look apologetic for liking biology.

Aunty Khan looked at me affectionately and started to convince my mother, "Well, at least she's not as bad as Sonia. She's been hiding in her room all summer and if I even mention prayers, she screams and locks her door. Eyes always glued to her cellphone—from morning to night—at least Nisha is reading books and not staring at her phone all day."

The comparisons had begun. Adults comparing me to other kids I had nothing in common with besides the tint of my skin. A child of poor immigrants is a racehorse. Our parents had brought us to this Canadian track to win the race—their race. Having thrown aside their country, their families, the familiarity of an ancient culture, the race was now everything. The feelings of their children, their thoughts, their ambitions and personal battles simply did not matter.

I was used to being talked about while sitting defenselessly, but it always made me squirm and blush. I took everything my mother said about me very seriously. Maybe all children do. Even if I didn't want to listen, whatever she said about me burrowed into the back of my head and always returned to whisper and create doubt.

"Nisha wants a phone, but I absolutely will not allow it," my mother shook her head. "You never know which boy's number will end up there."

The truth was she couldn't afford to buy me a cellphone. I wasn't interested in any boys and my mother knew that. My body had started to change and I was very conscious of my appearance and the last thing I wanted was to share it with anybody. I didn't look at boys and wore the baggiest and ugliest clothes, hoping they wouldn't look at me.

But they did. Clothes, no matter how bulky, would naturally fall and wrap around the shape of my body, accentuating all the juts and dips. I wanted to hide my body away from all eyes, but I couldn't forever conceal the vessel God gave me to travel the planet. That's all a body meant to me. My mother would often comment on my changing shape, which always left me close to tears because there was nothing I could possibly do about it. I just listened to her obediently when she told me what to wear.

"She is starting high school soon, correct?" Aunty Khan continued to talk about me without looking at me. "She needs to be very careful with high school boys."

My desperation to escape the conversation forced me to excuse myself. I quickly swallowed my food and put down my utensils. "Can I be excused to the washroom, Aunty Khan?"

"Yes darling, there's one right here downstairs by the entrance and a bigger one upstairs, darling."

"Yes, I remember, thank you." I left the table.

"Oh, Nisha?" Aunty Khan stopped me. "Why don't you go upstairs and tell Sonia to come down and join us? She's locked herself in her room as usual."

"Sure, Aunty, of course." I nodded with false enthusiasm.

"She is just so polite and mature," Aunty Khan gushed about me as I walked towards the door.

"No, she is a nightmare," my mother mumbled.

Her words always hurt me, but I knew her public criticism of me was her strange way of displaying humility. Maybe her true belief was that I was great—the perfect daughter—and she just couldn't show the world her immodest pride. At least that's what I told myself.

I walked slowly up the winding staircase where another foyer, about the size of a small hotel lobby, opened into the bedrooms. The walls were bare and the only light in the quiet hallway came from a large bay window across from where I was standing. Unlike the rest of the house, there were no lavish decorations or expensive carpeting on this floor. Guests were not welcome here.

Just the thought of seeing Sonia made me uncomfortable. I stood by the window for a moment to calm myself, taking in all the greenery from the massive backyard. All I could see was the green grass, the trees, and the flowers. All I could hear was the sound of my own breath. Sonia, no matter how rich and privileged, still had to spend her summer in this cemetery. There must've been moments when she felt completely alone. Maybe we had something in common after all.

I thought to myself I should hurry and greet her. It would be impolite not to. Bravely, I knocked on the bedroom door that had a rhinestone-encrusted "S" on it. I heard a faint "Go away, Mom!" I could never have addressed my mother that way. I told her it was me and a moment later the doorknob turned.

A bleached blonde Sonia stood on the other side in a bubble-gum pink robe with a sarcastic smile on her face. She looked both gaudy and exotic. Her face was surreally beautiful—a perfect match between proportion and symmetry—clearly the result of extreme luck and not her unfortunate-looking parents. Sonia knew she stood out and she knew she could have anything she wanted just by using a little creative flirting.

"Salam Alaykum," I smiled with my head involuntarily down, "I love the hair, Apu."

"Don't call me Apu. I'm not your fucking sister." She grabbed my hand and yanked me inside the room before suddenly releasing it and walking away, her slender silhouette glowing against the sun. "Come in. Shut the door."

Entering Sonia's bedroom was like stepping into the magical world of an eternally young child. This didn't look like the hiding place of an angry fifteen- or sixteen-year-old. Everything in it, from the walls to the velvet teddy bears on her bed, was in a shade of pink, cheetah print, sprinkled with glitter, or plated with rhinestones.

After taking in every sparkling corner of her room, I noticed a plate of pastries in her hand. She placed it on her bed and slid herself under the hot-pink duvet. She put her laptop on her legs and grabbed a chocolate-dipped donut to munch on.

"Y-your m-mom said you should come down and eat with us." I dared to interrupt her.

She chewed her mouthful slowly, refusing to look up from her screen until she was finished eating. I stood still in the awkward silence, afraid to take a step in any direction or breathe too loudly.

"It's so good." Sonia licked the chocolate off her manicured fingers as she stared at me temptingly. "Sit down."

"Wh-where should I sit?"

"Don't see a chair?" Her eyes led me to the pink leather task chair by her desk.

The desk was covered with papers and coloured pencils. The papers were covered with drawings. Nude female bodies in different configurations, all with a girl's expressionless face. The hair was yellow, the eyes empty brown circles, mouth missing. But they were striking. I couldn't take my eyes off them.

"I didn't know you were interested in art," I said with surprise.

"I'm not." Sonia's seductive stare switched into a cold glare. "My therapist told me to use art to express my emotions. She said it's better than burning buildings and killing cats."

I gaped.

"You'll believe anything, won't you?" Sonia rolled her eyes. "You're a gullible little girl, Nisha."

I ignored her tone and pretended to study her art. Some drawings were hidden under others and I dared to pull them out. These had white lilies at the feet of the naked girl, and unlike the other drawings, this girl's lips were turned downward. She looked sad.

"You're looking at those drawings very closely." She put aside her laptop and asked, "Are you a virgin, Nisha?"

I blushed and recoiled into the chair. Sonia was always inappropriate, but this question was bold even for her.

"You can tell me, I'm your Apu," she mocked. "Answer me . . . are you a virgin?"

"Of course!" I snapped and felt the need, almost reflexively, to remind her, "In our religion, that stuff doesn't happen until after marriage."

She broke into a giggle. "Is that what they're telling all the pretty girls in the hoods? Keep those legs closed until the expensive wedding? Keep your pearl pure and pristine and a rich prince might take you out of the sea?"

"No, that's what Islam tells us," I retorted indignantly.

Sonia composed herself and gave me an approving smile. "You seem like a true believer, Nisha—"

"—I am."

"And that makes you . . . " She stared at me so intensely, her eyes could have pierced through my clothes. " . . . very special."

"Why?" I sprung up from the chair and headed for the door.

"Because you're not pretending. You're actually innocent."

She peeled off her duvet, revealing a bare leg inside her robe. And before I could turn away I glimpsed slight stretch marks on her inner thigh where it met her red panties. A smirk had formed on her lips; she was amused by my discomfort.

"Do you know how many girls act so good and decent but secretively love every minute of it?" Sonia finished the last donut on her plate, licking the icing off her fingers suggestively again.

"Love every minute of what?"

"Sex."

She enjoyed that. She loved watching just how deeply she could offend me and leave me without words. I was beneath her, the bored rich girl, and she loved shaking me up for her entertainment.

"I should go downstairs now."

"You know what's sad about innocence, Nisha?" Sonia raised her voice as I rushed towards the door. "Once it's gone, it's gone forever. You can never have it back."

Sonia looked directly at me with her steely dark eyes. My palms, no longer sweaty but cold with apprehension, convinced me to leave immediately.

"I'm going to go downstairs now. Please come join us soon. My mom would love to see you."

"I'll come downstairs in a bit." Her tone suddenly became friendly. "You know, my brother would love to see you."

I was happy to change the topic and hid my fear by returning a stiff smile. "I hope Riad Bhai is doing well."

"Why don't you go greet him. After all, he is your 'brother'."

"He's here?"

Sonia nodded. "Go to the hall across and walk straight down. His bedroom is at the very end."

Growing up in a community where parties were gender-segregated, I knew it was highly inappropriate for girls and boys to mingle. Meeting a boy alone—and in his bedroom out of all places—was especially forbidden.

"A-are you sure I should do that? Isn't it rude?"

"No. But it is extremely rude not to greet your elders."

Sonia pushed her empty plate to the edge of the bed, signalling for me to fetch it. "Put this on my desk and go right now to my brother's room. Knock gently. Don't tell your mommy."

She adjusted her robe and returned to her laptop, ignoring me when I wished her a good day.

I revisited the hallway, overcome again by the miserable silence. I assumed my mother was too busy discussing how horrible I was to catch me going to Riad's room. She would've lost her mind if she found out I'd gone knocking on a boy's bedroom door.

I crept towards the room beyond the large window and bright sunlight, watching over my shoulder for my mother. I knocked on the door with a trembling fist, my feet itching to walk away as soon as possible.

Riad opened his door and gone was the image I had of him as a pimple-faced, try-hard teenager. He wore a simple white t-shirt with grey pajama pants. His hair was slightly shorter and gelled upwards. His skin was now smooth and clear with a sophisticated stubble. His aura of undeserved cockiness was replaced with a quiet refinement as he flashed me a friendly smile. Riad had become a man.

With my heart beating in my throat, I exhaled the words, "Salam Alaykum."

"Who are you?"

"It's me, Nisha." I jogged his memory, "Nisha Abbas, your Uncle Abbas's daughter."

Riad looked thoroughly confused as he moved his eyes from my face to my chest. After a moment of taking in my body, his eyes lit up.

"You're that Nisha?" He laughed in disbelief. "You look so . . . so grown."

I flushed and smiled at my shoes, and uttered quietly, "You look much older too. Nice to see you after all these years. I'll go downstairs now."

I was turning away to leave when he stopped me again with a resounding, "You look beautiful."

That could very well be the most powerful statement a rich, popular university guy could give to a bookish twelve-year-old girl. I was a smart kid—straight A's sort of kid—but the inexperience of my age was nothing any amount of science, math, or literature could alleviate. To hear I was beautiful from the mouth of an adult—a male adult with possessions I could only dream about meant so much to my adolescent mind—it validated me. He gave me much more than a fleeting compliment. He gave me worth.

"You-you really think so?" I asked.

"You're gorgeous!" Riad opened his door wide and motioned for me to come in. "Let's catch up. Tell me what you've been up to, Nisha."

"Our mothers are downstairs—"

"—Is it a sin to just talk for a minute?"

I looked around Riad's room. A large TV was mounted on the wall, playing some nature documentary about cheetahs. There were a few clothes sprawled out on the floor. His bedsheets were blue. His pillows were black. At that moment, there was nothing scary about Riad's room. But somehow, instinctively I knew the exact second the door closed behind me his true intentions. Maybe I was fully aware and just wanted to feel the presence of a man. It was exotic and mysterious to me: the stubble on the long face, the scent of aftershave, the security of the strong arms, as I imagined it. I only knew Tariq, my little brother who was a baby. My father was never home.

Riad began to tell me all about university and how to prepare in high school. He was quite funny and I remember laughing hysterically while keeping my eyes on the door. I kept turning to the shut door, just imagining fearfully my mother coming to break it down.

But my mother never came. A funny conversation about crazy professors turned into talk about love and sex. There are pieces of what happened that day that have gone missing in my mind. I know they're there—they would have to be because they glue together the events I can't force myself to forget— and I can't bear, even to this day, to search for them.

I saw a penis that day for the first time in my life. Not on a Greek statue, a cartoon, or porn that pops up on the Internet, but a real, in-the-flesh penis looking like a deformed limb.

"Is this not a sin?" I asked Riad several times with my eyes unable to meet his.

"The greatest sin," he paused to lift my chin up and force me to look him into his sincere eyes, "the greatest sin is to ignore your innermost desires."

I felt his hands unbutton my shirt and I knew this was far

from my innermost desires. I was a paralyzed child in shock and just like children do, I had tried to seek Riad's approval. His touch disgusted me to the point where I couldn't think about anything. But, surprisingly, the image of Sonia's room filled my mind. I disappeared into a world of glitter and sparkle, leaving my filthy body behind.

However, that was not the moment I first met evil. The moment was when my mind left the room of glitter and sparkle and entered Heaven. Here they all were, God, the angels, and billions of good dead people playing cards and golf in the clouds. They saw what was happening to me. They knew. And they did nothing.

From that moment on, the sun was a dying star and humans were just animals with oversized brains. My illusions dissipated and I understood the world.

Riad had climbed on top of me when I suddenly re-entered my body and looked to the door. It wasn't shut anymore.

Golden blonde hair shone from the door opening. With a satisfied grin, she watched me, my innocence, my self-love, my self-worth, and my childhood getting stolen. I locked eyes with her, upside down, and mouthed for her to help me. She winked and disappeared.

2

HE LIKES HIS EGGS free-range and brown, medium. Two whites, one yolk, always fried in olive oil and never runny. With that, a tall glass of cold grapefruit juice. The juice must fill two thirds of his glass—a half glass makes him feel like he's missing out on the vitamin C, and a full glass worries him that it'll spill on his suit.

Many say he's a complicated man, but I prefer to call him sophisticated. He never settles for anything less than what he wants. Indeed, I've always found his sharp decisiveness sexy, and that's why I agreed to marry him just four weeks after our fathers insisted we do.

I put a fork and a knife on a napkin next to his plate because he hates having his utensils touch his food before he can inspect their spotlessness. I take a seat at the table wearing nothing but the petal-pink satin robe he bought me while on a business trip recently. He loves seeing me in outfits he bought because those are the only ones he notices.

I woke up early today so I could do my makeup and hair the way he likes; no colour on the eyelids because that looks whorish, but a dusky rose on the lips because nothing is more

feminine. My dark hair is loose, straightened and parted to the
side because he thinks wavy hair looks unkempt and a middle
part makes me look old.

I don't doubt he still finds me attractive, but I know I've
become as worthy of his attention as our microwave or our
leather couch. Just like them, I have a function and I serve a
purpose, but I've become such an ordinary fixture of the house
that he barely sees me. And so I dress myself up when I need
his eyes on me like a desperate teenager stuffs her bra for her
acne-faced crush. I'm pathetic.

He is my husband, Azar. I used to be Nisha once upon a time,
but these days I'm more commonly called "Azar's wife." How
I became another person's possession is not a long, deep, or
even interesting story: I was a mid-twenty-something with no
career prospects and no assets except being born with a highly
coveted fair skin; Azar was rich. I bartered a promise of light-
skinned offspring for a life of luxury and comfort. It really was
that simple.

I was never in a hurry to get married, but my mother and
father caved into anticipated gossip from the Aunties. In our
community, where the grapevine is the official source of news,
rumours spread endlessly if you aren't married by a certain age.
My parents didn't want to hear that I was a closet lesbian; or
I couldn't produce babies; or I was promiscuous with a couple
of STDs; or I couldn't cook, kept my room filthy, and barely
showered. Or, the most common gossip, that I was already
secretly married to a white guy.

There is no empathy for those women of a certain age who
choose to stay single. And yet the life of a housewife is like
that of a farm animal: ridden at will like a horse, made to lay
eggs like a chicken, used for her milk like a cow . . . all while
attached to one, all-powerful, all-knowing farmer who leaves

her bleating at the barn while he enjoys the endless horizon of the field.

But here I am. And today is one of those days I really need my husband.

Every morning there is a moment of painful clarity soon after waking up that I can usually dodge by springing out of bed and breathing in the air of the present. Today I just couldn't leave my thoughts on my pillow. A flush of memories washed over me like a corrosive acid, stripping away the defensive veils of sweet ignorance I've spent all these years building.

My husband, unaware about the images of the past that haunt me every morning, is the best at helping me keep those memories at bay. When I'm with Azar, I magically succumb to all the expectations of normalcy. He is my normal. He is the only safety net to my frightening memories and thoughts free-falling into the universe.

"Good morning." A shirtless Azar walks in patting his freshly washed face with a towel. "You look pretty fancy."

A fresh whiff of bergamot and pineapple, the familiar scent of his cologne, wafts over me as he comes to stand tall and protective behind my chair. His fingers glide down my neck, gently massaging my shoulders.

"You noticed," I smile.

He holds my hands as I stand up to hug him, feeling his strong, sculpted body envelop mine. He works at his body just as hard as he works to keep his cars clean, put together his outfits, and have his hair and beard impeccably trimmed. Just like me, he is obsessed with the appearance of people and their things—an obsession everybody in our lives, from our parents to our circle of acquaintances share.

My mother taught me from early on that appearance is everything. It began in my teenage years, when beautifying myself became a way of holding up a shield to the world, but now I see in doing my makeup a magical route to transformation. I love decorating an empty face, washing away its flaws, highlighting its perfections, blending in brilliant colours and creating an entirely new, spectacular person. The glamour and confidence may wash off easily with soap, but I believe there is power in becoming somebody else—somebody better—even if it's just for a moment.

Indeed, Azar encouraged me to use this passion for beauty and turn it into a job. There are hundreds of makeup artists in our community, but he convinced me there's more than enough room for one more. With the high number of grandiose weddings for everyone to attend, there will always be somebody who needs to look like a Bollywood star for the night.

Without warning, Azar turned one of our guestrooms upstairs into a beauty salon, complete with lighted vanity mirrors and special chairs. Convinced that I would be fully booked every summer, he bought extra chairs for clients to wait their turn. Unfortunately those chairs remain empty most days: I may be great at blending eye shadows, but I'm terrible at marketing myself. Marketing oneself requires a lot of talking at parties and Azar's beautiful wife doesn't talk much—I just stand still, suck in my tummy, and focus on my great posture.

I was hoping my face would simply do my advertising for me since it usually receives the attention my voice doesn't. I wasn't born with this face; I've created it with the help of a surgeon, an aesthetician, a countless number of beauty products, and a semipermanent pouting expression I've perfected over the years. I hold this expression all the time in public and never allow my smile to reach my eyes. A full smile makes my cheeks look fat and my jawline less sculpted.

My features are naturally delicate and slight like my

mother's, and made perfectly symmetrical with the help of tattooed eyebrows and a nose job Azar gifted me two birthdays ago. My lips are large, my cheekbones high, my composed forehead is wrinkle-free and my chin stays prominent with the help of injections I pay hundreds of dollars several times a year. From my lipliner to my false eyelashes to the kajal around my impenetrable maroon eyes, I am always on, a breathing spectacle for envious and lustful stares.

I found out that flattery and a running mouth trump talent in the makeup business. Artists with permanent smiles, shelling out undeserved compliments get most of the clients. The unfriendly hermit types like me get whoever is desperate—the sympathetic housewives who book me out of geographical convenience or sheer pity.

Azar casually kisses my forehead and pulls away, but I pull him in closer. I run my fingers through the hair on his nape, begging for his attention. He gives in and grips my waist, kissing me intensely with his tongue. I feel like I've suddenly travelled five years back in time when I was a starry-eyed newlywed whose body tingled with every spontaneous kiss from this olive-skinned prince. He still has that effect on me sometimes, even after all those predictable days lived together.

"You know I have to go to work." He unglues his lips from mine and makes his way to the laundry room.

"I was thinking you could skip work today," I call after him.

"Why?" He returns in the white shirt I ironed for him this morning. "Are you ovulating?"

"No."

"No?" Azar laughs as he sits down for his breakfast. "So what could you possibly need me for?"

With my makeup business a failure, Azar thinks a baby will give me something to keep busy in this big house; a baby will fulfill all my needs; a baby will give us something in common with our friends because they're either all pregnant or new parents. I think I'd be the worst mother, but considering I do very little with my time, a baby would not be so bad a hobby. And, of course, it would please our mothers.

So, I've agreed to his latest venture, observing and inspecting my uterus like a science project the past six months. It's hard feeling sexy after peeing on ovulation strips but it's only when they prove positive that Azar wants me in lingerie, ready for him in the bedroom as soon as he's finished his dinner. We don't make love anymore; we make baby attempts.

Azar eats his eggs, one small, dignified bite at a time, avoiding eye contact with me.

"I'm not feeling well today," I admit.

"Is it your . . . " he pauses, his attention still on his breakfast, and sourly pushes out the word, "depression?"

As far as Azar knows, chronic depression is the only stain on his otherwise spotless wife. I never told him about what happened to me when I was twelve years old. I blame my sad days on nothing but a simple chemical imbalance. That white lie makes my imperfection just a mole on a clear face, instead of a burn. He can overlook it. He has no reason to ask any questions.

"Yes," I reply and plead with him, "I don't want to be alone today—"

"You're not alone. Aren't you doing Aunty Khaled's makeup this morning?"

"Yes, but if you stayed home, we could maybe drive to the Falls and eat at that nice Italian place by the rocks."

Azar rolls his eyes dismissively. "I have a job—I manage people, Nisha, I have responsibilities. If you kept yourself busy in the present like I do, you'd be too tired to even notice your depression."

"It's not something I can control, Azar."

"Of course you can. Everybody these days has depression, anxiety, or some other mental issue because they think too much. It's the overthinking that's driving everybody nuts. Stop thinking, start doing, and trust me, there is no time left in the day for self-pity and worrying about life."

"Sometimes it's that very mental issue that stops you from wanting to do anything," I mumble under my breath, afraid to disagree with Azar.

"Right. Did you call him?"

"Call who?"

"The doctor. The shrink I told you to call. He's one of the best in the city."

"I don't want to talk to some strange doctor. I want to talk to my husband."

"I understand." Azar gulps down his grapefruit juice and springs up from his chair, carelessly leaving his empty plate on the table for me to pick up. "I'll make you some tea before I go."

"Please, not the tea," I beg him pointlessly, "we're trying to have a baby."

"You aren't pregnant yet and it's the only thing that makes you feel good when you're having one of these days. I don't want to worry about you all day." He pauses, with concerned eyes. "I just want you happy, Nisha. I'll give you a very small amount."

I approve and see him impatiently take out the Red Powder from the cupboard as he heats up the water in the kettle. He leaves the Red Powder casually in a little jar next to our sugar and salt. The drug has become a normal part of my diet.

Nobody in the community, especially not Azar, likes to admit that the Red Powder is a narcotic. It's not sniffed, injected, or smoked, but added to drinks and sipped ever so elegantly at social gatherings. It's also not illegal if it's sold below a certain purity percentage. It was used in the past by Indian kings and queens and so it is deemed as traditional medicine. Its price, most importantly, is similar to the cost of saffron, making it an exclusive treat for the upper classes. And everybody, from stressed-out college students to my crazy mother-in-law, uses it to calm down.

I used to love a little of the Red Powder in my morning tea to quiet the loud voices in my head, but now the drug is beginning to frighten me. Azar insists I should have it every day—that it's not dangerous—but a single teaspoon no longer relaxes me. Even two teaspoons barely help my anxiety. I must use three to four teaspoons to change my reality and then, after two hours or so of absolute ecstasy, the dreaded hangover.

A Red Powder hangover is almost as bad as the very feeling I am trying to escape. There is no headache or vomiting, but a frightening sense of clarity. Being on the drug elevates you into a fantastically happy state; coming off it throws you back to the ground. You walk through the memories you tried to outrun, feel your pain in all its intensity. And there's no escape from the nightmare except to up the dosage.

Everybody, from the young professionals to the elders to the government, insists the Red Powder isn't addictive. They are wrong. I was able to choose when I wanted it, now it calls me. The weaker my moment, the stronger its call and the only happiness I know is when it's in me. I may not be physically addicted to the Red Powder, but I'm becoming addicted to the happiness it so cheaply gifts me.

Azar tells me to go to the living room where he follows me with my cup of tea. He sits me down on the couch, hands me the remote control for the TV and gives me permission to watch it all day if I finish my workout, cleaning, and his dinner.

He doesn't budge before I take a few sips of the tea. After he's satisfied with the amount I've drunk, he caresses my face quickly before starting his goodbye.

"I'm probably going to be late tonight."

"Again?" I am disappointed, but he shows no reaction.

I follow him to the foyer where he finds his silk socks laid out as he wants them on the entryway bench. Without thanking me, he hurriedly slips them on and finds his shoes.

"Like I told you, we have a big project due. Big client," he babbles, his hand on the doorknob. "This is how it's going to be the next few weeks. It's out of my control."

He has given me the tainted tea, which is his solution to all my problems, and he can now leave without guilt. He pecks me on the cheek and vanishes. I stare at the locked door, all alone with my thoughts and scared.

In the absence of Azar and all his rules, I can't stop thinking. I think and think, endlessly. I recall all that was said to me that hurt. I call up words of comfort that never came. All the useless prayers to a God who's not blind but most certainly deaf. My parents and my brother. About other people. Exploiters, liars, hypocrites. The two names that flash in my head like gaudy Las Vegas lights: Riad and Sonia.

I tell myself I'm Nisha, once upon a time a sprightly, grass-covered child who had a question for everything because curiosity was the engine of her soul. I'm still Nisha, but now Azar's well-groomed wife who looks forward to nothing but parties so I can show off my body and my artificial face and outfits and things. I'm a fresh coat of shiny paint on a piece of rotting wood. The sand races and the hourglass laughs. Every day I breathe in air, stuff my mouth, and flush the toilet as I wait, numb and dumb, for the end of consciousness and whatever waits or doesn't wait on the other side.

There is neither heaven nor hell on the other side because everybody is evil behind their masks. I don't believe God, who sees the bad in good people and the good in bad, cares to eternally reward all the hypocrites who are simply better actors than their neighbours.

Of course, I keep my mouth shut about what I really believe. I wear the invisible label that marks me as a Muslim, by birth and by association, and as Azar's wife. I am required to display piety, so he can remain popular in the community. And so while I observe the quiet wrongs in our friends and neighbours who backbite, treat their wives like maids, and their husbands like bank accounts, berate their children, show off their money, lie on their tax returns, I act especially outraged by those who nibble on bacon. They are the agreed-upon scapegoats because their sin is one the rest of us can easily avoid.

The Red Powder begins to overcome me and suddenly the thoughts stop racing. Everything in them is slow motion. I'm floating. The best thing about the Red Powder is that it doesn't only stop unwanted thoughts, it also stops negative feelings. Once those subside, I can carry on as a productive, good housewife.

My mind is clear and I'm happy as I begin to wriggle my toes into the broadloom. I've slipped into a pair of warm, fleece-lined slippers as I watch the carpet carefully. The fibres are like the fur on a cute animal. I notice the carpet is filthy and I get an urge to get up and grab the vacuum cleaner. With the help of the Red Powder, today won't be sixteen hours of me wallowing in self-pity.

I put my unfinished cup of tea aside and clear the floor for vacuuming. I remove Azar's slippers, his muscle magazines, and the empty can of kombucha he was drinking last night. I begin to feel a little annoyed at picking up all his stuff, but then hear the ding-dong of the doorbell. I realize Aunty Khaled is here to have her makeup done. I wonder what reason one would have to want to be glammed up at eight in the morning on a weekday, but I am happy she's giving me her company.

I open the door to see a beaming Aunty Khaled with a floral hijab loosely wrapped around her head. She wraps her arms around me and pulls me into her ample, fleshy self to kiss me on my cheeks. Any other time I'd feel violated—there are few things I hate more than being touched by anybody other than Azar and my own fingers—but the Red Powder dulls my disgust. The small amount I take allows me to tolerate the feel and scent of another human being. Maybe a larger amount would make me enjoy it, but I'm not taking chances yet.

"I'm so happy you're free, Nisha, my daughter!" Aunty Khaled grins. "I called around and nobody could see me this early."

I smile and tell her the hour is not an issue, ignoring the awkwardness of her just admitting I was her last choice.

"You're truly a lifesaver." Aunty Khaled removes her hijab and kicks off her slides.

"What's the event this morning, Aunty?" I ask.

"Oh, w-well," a guilty Aunty Khaled looks at me like a child expecting a scolding, "I'm going to the mosque for a funeral."

"You want your makeup done for a funeral?" I raise a brow, I've never had this request before.

"Yes. I know it sounds very unnecessary, but this funeral will have guests I haven't seen in a decade. These people talk a lot, and I don't want them to go back home to wherever they come from and tell everybody I look like . . . " Aunty Khaled pauses and goes on, " . . . that I look like an ugly old lady."

"You're in no way an ugly old lady," I reassure her.

She forces a smile and I notice her chipped, curry-stained

nails and the fading orange henna clinging desperately at her grey hair roots. She doesn't believe me.

"I don't need any fancy colours or red lipstick—just get rid of this," Aunty Khaled angrily points to her eyebrows where a few grey strands stick out.

"Sure. Just soften up and polish the face a little—a very natural look? I can do that." I invite her to come upstairs to my studio.

Aunty Khaled follows me, on the way complimenting my colour choices for the living room deco and how clean I keep my home. There isn't a hint of sarcasm or critique in her tone and that's why she's one of my favourite Aunties. I wouldn't mind replacing my mother and mother-in-law with this woman.

She slows down when we reach the staircase and notices the ascending framed pictures on the wall. The oldest one in the rising row is one of Azar and I on our honeymoon, huddled together in the balcony of our hotel with the vivid blue background of the Aegean Sea competing with our beaming smiles, our twinkling eyes. We spent most of that trip in our hotel room, mesmerized by each other's bodies.

The most recent one is from Venice taken two years ago, where we force a grin in the middle of St Mark's Square, pretending we don't have pigeon shit on our sandals. We spent a lot of that trip fighting about how his eyes kept wandering towards the fair-skinned, dark-haired Italian women.

I continuously forgive Azar his wandering eyes. After our parents had introduced us, he had bravely admitted to me on our first date that it was difficult for him to imagine only having sex with one woman for the rest of his life. He felt it was unnatural and no great man in history had only one woman in his life. Azar, in his mind, I thought sarcastically, was so great he deserved his own harem. This was the reason why, he explained, he was still unmarried at the ripe age of thirty, which made him a dinosaur in the bachelor pool, according to his mother. However, since his mother had now convinced him that he was an old man, he had promised to change and settle down for the right woman.

I believed him wholeheartedly. I was twenty-six and had also been told by my mother that I was old. She had convinced me that if I didn't settle down right there and then, no man of quality would want me in a couple of years. Desperately wanting to please my mother, stop being a financial burden on my overworked father, and move somewhere better than their nest, I forced myself to be ready for marriage. It couldn't be that bad—the expensive engagement ring, the magnificent wedding outfits, the exotic honeymoon—it was every young woman's dream. I also believed that Azar had shed himself of his old ways and reached a certain level of maturity.

Before he slid the five-figure diamond ring on my finger, I promised never to bring up his past and to trust him from then on. He knew my family was modest, he knew I had barely passed university, he knew I didn't have any career ambitions and couldn't hold a job for more than a year—and he took me as I was. I saw pity in his eyes, but I also saw acceptance. And I loved him for that.

We were not perfect, and that knowledge was the superglue of our marriage. A woman like me, mentally unstable with a nonexistent future, was not supposed to marry somebody wealthy, handsome, and popular. A man like Azar, admittedly a player, was not expected to be burdened with a wife and children. We were two abnormal people with a chance at a normal life.

But secrets are like hidden fruits: sweet at taste, sweeter than usual because they are yours, but then they rot and reek because you forgot where you stashed them. Sooner or later the stench is everywhere and inescapable. Azar and I forgot the promises we made to each other and now all we smell is the foul odour. There is no hiding it that my husband still looks at other women and I'm a traumatized lunatic who'd benefit from therapy. There is no hiding that perhaps we should've worked on ourselves a little more before becoming one.

But we have an image to uphold to the hundreds of people who witnessed our wedding. We must perpetuate the image of Azar and Nisha, the perfect married couple whose eyes forever sparkle when they look at each other. Our love is enviable; it is the happy ending of fairy tales. As singles we were forgettable. Together, we are seen in our community. We are liked and included, treated as special.

"What a beautiful life together," Aunty Khaled concludes after she's finished fawning over the pictures and we step into the upstairs foyer. "There is no greater blessing than a happy marriage. God bless you and Azar."

I nod and blush in anticipation of a baby-related question, but Aunty Khaled quietly follows me to the studio. The lights are off as she eagerly sits down on one of the salon chairs, facing away from the mirror. Her thinning hair sits in a bun above her nape. She takes off the hair band and I watch her long tangled strands fall over her slumped shoulders. Without looking in the mirror, she runs her fingers over her scalp a few times before redoing the exact same bun in the exact same place on her head and then announcing that she's ready.

I draw the curtains to let in some natural light and turn around to a striking vision. The sunlight has washed away the dark hollows under Aunty Khaled's eyes and highlighted her wonderfully straight and narrow nose. I don't notice the grey in her eyebrows or the endless lines of worry on her forehead because her glowing bronze eyes capture all my attention. I wonder if this is how she glowed once upon a time, before having her three sons and spending all her days in a hot kitchen. "What is it?" Aunty Khaled smiles.

"Nothing." I smile back as I plan how I will recreate this youthful glow with my makeup products. "You look radiant."

I don't know if I'm suddenly inspired by the sunlight, but somehow, I know exactly what to do to bring out the buried beauty of Aunty Khaled's face. Enthusiastically and in a rush of creativity I grab my cosmetic cases and lay out the products and the brushes on the table. But then, as I'm about to wipe Aunty Khaled's face clean and begin my art, I remember I didn't finish my Red Powder.

Now the task that seemed so easy just a few seconds ago suddenly feels impossible. I can't bring my hands to continue.

"Let me just go downstairs and grab my tea," I blurt and head towards the door.

Aunty Khaled says something behind my back, but I ignore it and rush down the stairs. On the way a smiling Azar in the vacation photos watches me. I feel him staring at my back as I turn around and reach for the teacup on the living room table. I chug the Red Powder down as he wished.

He can't be blamed for wanting me to be normal. I came into his life with my secrets shrouded, my past completely unspoken. All he can do is accept that I can't ever be like his friends' bubbly, bouncy wives. He knows every corner of me is darkness even on the sunniest days, and even when the joke is truly hilarious my smile is forced. All he can do is mix in the Red Powder into my tea, drug me up to keep me somewhere between comfortable and content.

All he can do, to prevent my sorrow from steeping into him and interrupting his perfect life, is to keep me high.

3

A RAPE BECAME a relationship.

But then again, all rapes, like murders, become a relationship between two people. Somebody you'd never want to touch you or even be in your life can force themselves upon it to become the subtext in your biography. They take over your mind, direct the choices you make every day, how you treat the people you do love—the ones you want in your life.

I became a recluse as soon as I started grade eight, harbouring the secrets of the summer, when Sonia would lure me upstairs in their house to be touched by her brother again and again. The secret was heavy enough but the shame that accompanied it nearly broke me. I was afraid to make new friends, stuck only to the girls I'd known since kindergarten. I didn't speak to Tariq or my mother unless they asked me something. Nobody was allowed close to me. I no longer made eye contact. I didn't want anybody to see through me.

I spent my days hiding in the solitude of my room, wanting to get lost in other people's worlds. I wanted to escape into somebody else's life—anybody else's life—so I inhaled celebrity tabloids and biographies. I lost myself on the Internet, reading rags-to-riches stories about beautiful Cinderellas who had nothing but with the help of miracles now lived in mansions filled with expensive dresses, diamonds, jewels. Here was lowly I reading about happy they, surrounded by beautiful, glitzy things.

Gone was my desire for knowledge; I wanted to acquire makeup, jewellery, stylish modern clothes. I starved myself and spent all my lunch money at the mall, and sometimes I stole. Stealing pretty things and getting away with them gave me a rush no science book ever could.

I felt powerful in my mask of heavy makeup and in revealing Western clothes that I'd change into at school. The power to turn off my mind and dress up as somebody else might have saved my life. My mother seemed proud about the makeup. To her I was just becoming a woman, enhancing my grooming routine. While she encouraged me to borrow her lipsticks, she didn't even once ask why I spent all day in my room.

In between my search for celebrities and things, I'd read Riad's e-mails. I still didn't have a cellphone, so he'd send me e-mails almost every day. He'd write about all the dirty things we did, send me links to his favourite porn videos, but he would also ask how school was and profess his love for me. He'd always sign off by telling me he missed me, and I would reply that I missed him too—even after he'd bit my nipple so hard it bled. Yes, I even told my rapist that I loved him.

Why?

I had turned thirteen in August and been given a hefty choice by the universe: I could cry my eyes out every night in the dark, tell everybody Riad raped me and hope they would believe me, tell my religious parents I wasn't a virgin, admit to myself that with all my intelligence, my talents, my beauty, my thoughts, my ability to love, I was still just flesh to be preyed upon, consumed to fill the most basic of needs and then tossed away like toilet paper . . . or I could smile and pretend like I had a rich older boyfriend.

I chose the latter because nobody wants to be a victim. Victims are shunned. I'd cockily chat with my friends about my mystery boyfriend. I never told them his real name. I didn't say a word about sex. I regaled them with fairy tales about gifts that were never bought, sweet words that were never said, dates in exotic places that never happened. In an act of survival, I twisted my deepest source of shame into my most salient point of pride.

The male attention was satisfying too. Before Riad's incessant barrage of compliments on my everchanging body, I was ashamed even to look at myself naked in the mirror. I used to think my maturing curves were obscene. I used to hide under layers of ugly, baggy clothing because my parents had convinced me that good Muslim girls could control lustful infidel boys simply by dressing modestly. They were so busy protecting me from strangers and the immorality of the West, they never cared to protect me from the familiar.

Once Tariq and I returned to school again in September, my mother stopped dragging us to the Khans', and so I didn't get to see Riad anymore. I remember how anxious and nervous my classmates were about starting grade eight: the last voyage before high school and then finally adulthood. And then there was me, walking with a bounce in my step the first day of class. School had rescued me and I wished summer break never returned.

I may have been freed from seeing and being touched by Riad once school started, but he remained in my life. His e-mails continued but began to escalate in their graphicness. At first, the porn links he sent were just of young women and men having passionate sex—the obvious continuance of what would happen between a Bollywood hero and heroine after they've danced and sang together with the tip of their noses touching. I felt naughty watching those videos but they were so predictable. They showed things that I had also done.

But gradually what he sent me were miles beyond my imagination. They frightened me.

There would be a girl who'd supposedly just turned eighteen and a brute of a man or several men whose faces were not shown. The girl would be tossed around, slapped, choked, or made to stand and arch her back in impossible positions. She had no way to protest because her mouth was constantly being used. But even when she had a moment to breathe, or the only expression on her face was unconcealable agony, she would never say no.

Riad called this wholehearted acceptance of bodily pain and humiliation a form of dedication, a provable symbol of commitment. If I loved him as much as he loved me, I should submit my body to him limitlessly. I should meet his best friends during the winter break and prove to him—and all of them—just how deep my love truly was.

I was shocked, yet continued, somewhere far in the back of my mind, to plan how to be with him in December. I was planning something I knew I would never do, like a melodramatic person Googling to find out the least painful way of committing suicide, just for the curiosity of it. I thought if I did anything for Riad—any sexual act, no matter how revolting to me—he might want to marry me.

And maybe God would love me again because I'd marry the man who took my virginity. Maybe it wasn't too late for me to enter Heaven.

Life and school continued as I forced myself to forget my past with Riad and focus on my future with him. I embraced this new reality that I had created, in which he would soon marry me and save me from this life of poverty. I'd no longer have to crave my father's presence, compete for my mother's affection, or endure their thunderous fights. One day I'd have my own family with Riad: a normal family that eats dinner together, laughs together, talks to each other without screaming.

The further in I time moved away from that horrible summer, the braver I became with my imaginary love story.

"Do you have a picture?" They would ask me.

I only had pictures of his nude body, but always with his head cropped off; just like his elusive sister Sonia, he was nowhere to be found on social media.

"Yes, I do." I lied once. "I'll show you after class."

One day I went to the school library and printed out some handsome stranger's headshot off the Internet. The boy in the picture had all the features I found attractive; he looked nothing like Riad. With an arrogant smirk on my face, I presented the picture in the girls' locker room. Disbelief and derision. I don't believe you! It's a fake! They laughed. The quiet, meek Nisha transformed into a witch, I got into such a rage, punching and shoving and screaming, that the teacher had to step in to stop the commotion.

That was the first and last time I'd ever been scolded by a teacher.

A few days after the locker-room incident, Riad's e-mails came to an abrupt stop. I checked and rechecked my inbox constantly, frantically, not understanding why he had suddenly stopped writing to me.

I'd been used and tossed away. He'd said he loved me, and even though in my heart of hearts I had known that was a lie, in my young, one-dimensional thirteen-year-old mind, the word *love* placated every action. My father abandoned me for work because he *loved* me. My mother controlled my every move because she *loved* me. Riad raped me because he *loved* me. The love was gone now that he had disappeared. I was angry. I was so angry that I couldn't feel anything else anymore. Every other emotion had been sucked out of me and replaced with a searing, deadening, deep rage. Alone in my room, I had to accept the new me: a girl with no sympathy, curiosity, or gratitude left in her for anyone. Alone and angry in the dark, I became numb.

"What happened to your boyfriend?" friends asked.

"We broke up," I'd say robotically. "He's got a job in England."

I knew they were laughing behind my back. They were no longer my friends anyway, because I didn't want friends. We'd still hang out at school and we'd still talk on the phone but I never truly listened to their words anymore. Their problems, which involved forgetting to do homework or not understanding an algebra question, didn't match mine. I was nothing like them. They were still sweet, compassionate little girls.

One December evening, I dressed up like I was going to just another party. I had taken hours to curl my hair and do my makeup impeccably. This was my first time attending a fancy banquet hall and I was determined to show myself off. My mother wrapped a turquoise saree around my now womanly body and a few of her thin gold necklaces around my neck. The saree was hiked up far beyond my navel so as not to show my stomach, of course, but there was nothing she could do about the sexy look of the sheer fabric.

"Hurry up, we're going to be late!" my mother yelled at my dad, who was trying to find a tie to match his suit.

My father had only one suit, a dark grey one he had brought from back home, but when he wore it, he looked like the richest man in the world. He wasn't very tall or imposing, but he had a certain charm and mystery about him that shone through when he wasn't wearing his usual jeans and checkered shirts.

My mother slapped some gel into a complaining Tariq's hair and began combing it back.

"It's sticky and disgusting!" Tariq cried.

"Quiet!" she shouted, at the same time securing the end of her maroon saree.

My father forced himself into his dress shoes, mumbling under his breath, "Who gets engaged in this cold?"

"You should just be happy they invited us," she barked at him. "It's not like you ever take us anywhere as fancy!"

"I took you with me to Canada—what more do you want?" he retorted.

The profanities flew back and forth as I happily sprayed on my mother's perfume. Tariq and I were so used to our parents' fighting that it was just background noise now.

I slipped into my heels, feeling beautiful and regal, and we were finally all ready to leave. Stepping into the dark hallway with its stained carpet and curry smell, I smiled in a complete state of bliss, my parents following behind promising to kill each other, and Tariq in front, using his own spit to wipe off his hair gel.

Nothing was going to stop me from enjoying Riad's engagement party.

He had disappeared because he was getting married. Every painful and violent thing he had done to me just months ago, all the perverted imagery he'd made me watch just weeks before, all the promises of love he'd given me as his plaything had disappeared into a huge, sweeping cloud of nothingness. Because he could, he simply stepped out of my life as if he had never been in it at all.

Snow leapt around in the ferocious winter wind. As we arrived, the string lights outside the banquet hall twinkled brightly through the flurries like stars. I was lost in the magic of the night. I didn't care whose romance it was celebrating.

My father dropped my mother and me at the entrance in an appearance of stylish formality and we proceeded to the entrance. We opened the door with the gilded handle and followed a red carpet into a marble-floored foyer with a row of magnificent chandeliers cascading down from the tall ceiling. Classic Bollywood love songs blared from behind a large doorway that was decorated with an arch of fresh pink and white roses. My mother and I were stunned by the sheer elegance and for some moments we stood awkwardly in the foyer, our arms crossed, looking for a familiar face amidst the Khans' sea of important friends.

I watched the women and girls who were lucky enough to afford professional hair and makeup and felt my mother and I looked rather underdressed in our old sarees with few embellishments. There were girls my age wearing the most stunning clothes: silk sarees, lehengas, and salwar kameezes in every colour imaginable, swaying fluidly with every step, lights striking every individually stitched rhinestone and sequin. They looked beautiful and I felt ugly.

As we waited for my father and Tariq, we took in the decorations to make ourselves appear busy. Right beside the arch of roses, there was a large easel with a decorative foam board that read "Congratulations to Riad & Afreen."

Without ever seeing her, I was sure Afreen was the most beautiful girl ever with impossibly large breasts, a butt like two soccer balls pressed together, teeth as white as eggshells, and shiny onyx hair flowing to her kneecaps. She must've had otherworldly beauty to convince somebody as shallow and horny as

Riad to marry her. I'm sure she was a virgin too, an untouched special little pearl—another jewel the Khans could boast about adding to their many possessions.

My father and Tariq came to the foyer at the same time as a familiar face appeared from inside the main hall.

"Welcome, welcome!" A beaming Aunty Khan glimmering in heavy gold jewellery threw her arms around my mother. "And, of course, As-salamu alaykum."

"What an amazing hall," my mother fawned, "it's absolutely beautiful. Thank you and bhai so much for having us."

"You look beautiful, my daughter!" Aunty Khan kissed my cheeks before pulling my mother towards the main party room. "Come, I must introduce you to some people before it gets busier!"

My mother disappeared with Aunty Khan to mingle with important strangers. I looked to my father to take me to our table, but he told me to wait while he and Tariq used the men's washroom. Standing awkwardly alone in the middle of the chatting crowds, I searched desperately for a familiar face. And cringed when I found one.

Sonia, almost unrecognizable, showed up out of nowhere. She had tied her blonde hair into an updo and wore a very covering salwar kameez which was, surprisingly, a conservative olive green and not hot pink. Her makeup was glamorously subdued and if I didn't know who she really was, I'd have confused her for a kind, modest person.

I watched her smiling and welcoming the guests. Nobody here knew what she really was. By now, I became an expert at taming the savage beast that was my anger. I wrestled it down; I sat on it with all my might, but it still appeared in the form of a sudden pain in my stomach. The more I watched people smiling at and admiring beautiful Sonia, the worse the pain stung.

I couldn't look at Sonia's smug face for too long because then I might've keeled over in front of all those beautiful people and died right there on the floor. We acknowledged each other with a nod, but once my father returned and I tried to walk past her, she suddenly turned and hugged me like we were best friends.

"I'm so happy to have you here, Nisha." She looked straight into my face, her hands resting on my shoulders, and asked loudly, "Are you happy for my brother?"

"I'm very happy for your brother," I answered coldly, refusing to show her my feelings.

She leaned in again for a hug and whispered mockingly into my ear, "Did you think he was going to marry you? Nice saree, slut."

Sonia turned swiftly, smiled in the direction of my father and Tariq, and disappeared to greet more guests. Tears welled up in my eyes and I found my mother somehow and told her I had to use the washroom. She dismissed me, not even noticing my sadness because she was so busy admiring Aunty Khan and her rich friends' dazzling outfits. She was so busy speaking to these pigs in lipstick that she didn't react at all to me poking her back. I needed comfort. I needed comfort so desperately I thoughtlessly expected it from my self-righteous, emotionally illiterate, social-climbing mother.

Alone in a washroom stall, I found comfort in one of my beloved, inanimate objects: a tube of mascara. Mascara doesn't let you cry. I piled it on and deterred myself from crying by imagining re-entering the party hall with black goo all over my face.

Once all the girls outside the stall had finished taking their selfies and I'd collected myself, I slowly made my way out of the washroom. The foyer was nearly empty now except for a few kids running around and the workers scrambling back and forth. I heard loud applause and cheers from the main hall and hurried in.

Hundreds of people stood up and clapped for a beaming, debonair Riad clad in a black tuxedo, strutting across the dance floor with a bouquet of flowers in his hands. A ballad in Urdu about eternal love played as the soft white spotlight followed him to a stage with a backdrop of silk curtains. On one of the two red and gold armchairs placed a good distance apart on the middle of the stage, Riad's bride sat with her veiled head turned down.

The crowd roared their congratulations as I stood alone in a corner, watching Riad's horrible acting unfold. Basking in the applause, he got on one knee like a gentleman and handed his fiancé the flowers.

I was surprised to see that the girl on stage was not the great voluptuous beauty I had imagined. She was incredibly young, and her skin was nearly paper white—or at least her makeup made it appear that way. Whiteness was the only beauty standard for many in this room. She was hardly the busty, long-haired, doll-like porn star he had showed himself to be obsessed with. She was chubby with an asymmetrical face, no curvature on her chest, and her hair was hidden under a hijab.

But maybe she had been his ideal woman all the time. Maybe Riad didn't want to marry his fantasy but rather keep it as private as the depraved things he had done to me in the privacy of his bedroom. I was a dirty secret; his wife was his public representation of himself and his oh-so-important family. His wife couldn't be the sexual inferno of his inner demon; she had to be a virtuous, religious, unsexy deflection.

He sat next to his fiancé and his hordes of friends rushed on the stage to take pictures. I scanned the room quickly and found the table where my family were sitting. On my way I recognized and smiled at many of the Aunties and Uncles my parents were friends with. Some of them had daughters my age or slightly younger. I took their faces in, stupidly looking for something that might hint that Riad had done to them what he had to me. But if they had been through the same thing as me, they'd have on a mask too.

"She's not that pretty," I whispered bitterly to my mother.

"Who cares?" she shrugged. "She's a medical student. Her brother is a doctor. Her father is a doctor. Her uncle is a doctor."

My father added, "Her mother's father is a doctor too."

My parents looked at Afreen with awe, thoroughly impressed by the number of medical degrees in her family. There was nothing the Khans loved more than impressing others, so it was clear that Afreen was hand-picked by Aunty and Uncle Khan to be Riad's wife.

"Should we go up and take a picture with them?" my mother asked me.

"No," I refused.

I did not want to lock eyes with Riad. Luckily, our table was far from both the stage and the buffet tables, so I found it easy to hide.

My mother nagged and eventually convinced my father to go with her to take a picture. I was left alone with Tariq. I looked around everywhere except where Riad was and suddenly captured a pair of eyes staring at me.

It was Sonia who glared at me from a few tables behind. She sat with around ten of her chatty girlfriends, all in their late teens and immaculately made up. Their designer purses were scattered around their table, and they all had their cellphones out, taking pictures and laughing loudly.

I turned away, thinking our eyes had just met accidently, but when I turned back, she was still staring at me. This time, she leaned over to the girl next to her and whispered something in her ear. That girl was now staring at me too and smirking. My heart throbbed with panic and I turned away, red-faced. I couldn't believe Sonia would tell somebody what Riad had done to me. There was no way she'd admit to anybody that her brother was a rapist, a pedophile, a criminal. So what was she telling that girl?

I dared to turn around and look at their table again. Now all pairs of false-lashed, judgemental eyes were watching me with disgust. They snickered behind their manicured fingers and shook their heads.

I sprung up from my chair and rushed towards the exit. Now there were at least ten people who knew my most painful secret. Ten people could tell another twenty people. Twenty people could tell hundreds more until the word travelled back to me and right into my parents' ears.

"Where are you going?" Tariq called after me.

I ignored his sweet boyish voice and hurried to the washroom. I would spend the rest of that night locked up between the four walls of a washroom stall. My face burned with panic and shame. I knew I could never see these people again. I couldn't see anybody from this party ever again. I just wanted to spend the rest of my life alone.

4

"THE SHETTLES METHOD will guarantee us a boy," Azar begins as he zooms out of our driveway at a clearly illegal speed. "I talked to some guys at work; it worked for them."

I hug a freshly ordered banana bread in my lap as I nod and pretend to be happy to talk about babies first thing in the morning. He will drop me off at Simi's house on his way to work. Simi is one of his best friends' wives, and her plump face is one I'm used to see often. Now she's pregnant.

"All we have to do is make sure we have sex close to the day you ovulate. The boy sperm is faster than the girl sperm, so it'll just race up to the egg and win the competition."

We reach the main road and move slowly through the morning rush. As he talks I gaze enviously outside the window at the people in the other cars. I wish it were possible to transfer myself into another body, be somebody else. I wish I could hear whatever song is playing in their car or whatever conversation they're having. I wish I could hear anything right now but baby talk.

Today is a good day. On a good day, I don't desperately need the Red Powder to stop the bad memories, but the problem with not focusing on the past is that it usually means I'm focusing on the future. And I don't see an adorable giggling baby in my crystal ball; I see stretch marks, deformed breasts, torn stomach muscles. I see years of catering to all the demands of a screaming, helpless, diaper-wearing human being. I see myself squeezing my fat post-baby body into my clothes like minced meat into a sausage casing, in my vain attempts to get Azar to pay attention to me.

"Look at this fucking turtle!" Azar honks at the elderly man in the car in front of us before rudely cutting him off. "And of course I'm fucking running out of gas."

I've learned not to speak when Azar is angry. I quietly watch his proud profile as he simmers down. He curses himself, his lips moving without pause beneath his stately Roman nose. His umber eyes sparkle behind his designer sunglasses as he swerves so speedily into a gas station that the banana bread almost flies off my lap.

"Are you listening to me?" He turns to me while we wait behind a line of cars.

"Yeah, you were talking about the Shettles Method?"

"Yes, the method is why it's super important that you keep using the ovulation strips. If we don't know when your egg is here, we will be having sex way too soon."

"And what's wrong with that?"

"Well, if we do it too soon, we will end up with a girl."

"And what's wrong with a girl?" I confront him carefully.

I never quite understood the community's preference for baby boys. A screaming, drooling little horror is a screaming, drooling little horror no matter what's between its legs. I can grudgingly justify the elders' perspective: they come from a place and time where uneducated daughters were married off and breadwinning sons inherited vast amounts of land and multiple properties—a sexist rule born from religious texts and a culture that withheld opportunities from women so they could easily be controlled. But what's the excuse here and now? My husband hates when people disagree with him or challenge his views. He's the top manager at a software company and is used to his underlings always nodding their heads. If he is pushed far enough, a frightening monster that I barely recognize rips through his skin. His eyes redden, the veins on his forehead protrude, and his lips form a sinister smirk before he verbally assassinates whoever disagrees with him. He has a talent for noticing people's deepest insecurities and will always get his opponents to shut up by throwing their weaknesses into their faces.

"Nothing is wrong with a girl," Azar explains mockingly. "But the first born should be a man. He can protect his younger siblings. Men protect."

I snicker at Azar's nonsense. Many men protect, and many men hurt, rape, cheat, battle, kill, rob, and join politics.

"What's so funny about that?" he retorts.

I know better than to argue with him.

"You're being sexist," I accuse him in the least offensive tone I can manage. "You're assuming boys will just automatically choose to protect girls. But they could just as well choose to use their strength for something cynical. A daughter could easily choose to protect herself."

"I didn't know you were so brilliant," Azar uses his childish sarcastic tone. "Maybe you should've gone to law school."

Of course he wastes no time reminding me of my deepest failure. My parents encouraged me to become a lawyer, but I only survived university because of prescription antidepressants. Behind my confident mask, I always doubt my intelligence. I worry that I'm truly and simply stupid. The only reason Azar knows this about me is because I told him once through tears while we were in the privacy of our bedroom, high on the Red Powder and drunk on wine. He wasn't supposed to remember.

"I'm sorry," I back off and he wins again. "I would just be happy with a healthy child . . . boy or girl."

"Yes, them coming out with a beating heart and working eyes is the most important thing, but let's try for a boy because we can."

I nod and sigh with relief at the return of peace. The silence grows louder as we keep waiting.

Azar finally drives up to an available pump and undoes his seatbelt. He leans over and gives me a peck on the cheek. That's his way of apologizing for making me feel small. I kiss him back, swallow my pride, and accept his apology because there aren't really any other options. I'll never be bigger than him.

Azar scrambles out of the car, not noticing his cellphone falling out of his pocket. I watch it sit there naked and exposed in the leather seat, his entire life compressed into this tiny metal rectangle. A good wife should not be interested in its contents. A good wife, like an unbothered house cat, should just be busy with her toys while she waits for her poor owner to come home from the cruel outside world.

But this cat is curious. I want to know all about Azar's world. I want to know all about this project that keeps him coming home late. All he ever talks about now is kids; I don't know much about what's happening in his head except that he wants a son. I decide, for the few minutes that Azar is busy with the gas nozzle behind our tinted car windows, that I will be a bad wife for the first time in five years.

He doesn't know that I know the code to unlock his phone,

having looked over his shoulder enough times at the dining table while running around behind him to the kitchen and back. I grab his phone quickly and see sixteen new messages—at least he wasn't lying about being busy. Without clicking on the messages, I can see the profile pictures and names of whoever sent them. I know most of these people, they're just his friends and the guys from his workplace, but there's one blonde-haired face that stands out. I don't recognize this girl.

Her name is Linda, and she has sent my husband two messages. She doesn't look any older than twenty-five. She's pretty. But so are all the other freshly graduated, starry-eyed interns at Azar's company. But how many interns have the big boss's number? Maybe she's not just an intern. Maybe I'm making assumptions because she's young and pretty. She could be a manager too. Yes, she must be a newly hired manager because I haven't seen her at any of the office Christmas parties.

I decide not to read Linda's messages because there's nothing to worry about. I carefully place the phone exactly where I found it. He returns to his seat just a minute after, and I find myself gulping with guilt. I grab his hand and place it lovingly on my chest for a moment.

"What was that for?" He takes my hand and kisses it before starting the car. We speed away towards the highway.

"Nothing," I shrug. "I just love you."

"I love you too."

Azar blasts his playlist which consists, ironically, of hardcore 90s and early 2000s gangster rap. I always found his taste in music odd for someone who lives in tailored dress pants and grew up miles away from the ghettos of Toronto. Azar had an ideal childhood in the suburbs, the type of life I would often daydream about when I stood in my mother's tiny balcony, feeling close to her through her plants. While my young days consisted of school and watching TV at home, Azar had enjoyed hockey lessons, neighbourhood barbeques, cottaging, and all kinds of other fun activities that cost money. He was a private school preppie who spent his summers in camp and winters vacationing in Dubai.

Maybe he loves this kind of music because street life and poverty are exotic to him. And that's why he chose me to be his wife when he had so many other choices. I was something out of the ordinary; something thrilling and novel to explore.

But now he's made me a permanent fixture in his world and I'm just another unexciting extension of him. He has given me everything I used to dream about, and so at some point I just stopped dreaming.

I check myself out in my compact mirror. I look the way Azar wants me to look when mingling with his friends' wives. I've left the red lipstick and mink eyelashes at home because looking too sexy is a quiet threat; bait for being shunned and gossiped about. I'm wearing a trendy beige fitted sleeveless bodysuit but covering my arms and my figure with an ankle-length cotton duster.

When it's just Azar and I drinking cocktails at the hottest downtown restaurants, I'm encouraged to show my skin, to show off some cleavage and even thigh. He loves that his Muslim wife can compete with sexy-looking Western women, has a body other men would desire. That's another one of our secrets, of course.

We exit the highway and approach Simi's house, which like ours is in a secluded residential area; her in-laws are not too far away. Indeed, there isn't much difference between Azar and his friends.

They are all well-dressed, well-educated men, perfectly groomed, with healthy bank accounts and in love with the sounds of their own voices. Their wives are all bouncy, pretty, politically correct, modestly dressed phonies with a degree they threw away as soon as they got the ring and a fantasy life on social media as "feminists" and "social activists." They spend their days convincing themselves that they *love* and *choose* to stay home while itching and begging for the outside world to acknowledge their daily posts about cooking, gardening, and baby advice that nobody asked for.

I'm sure Azar and I don't look any different to those who don't know our secrets. Maybe I'm wrong and all these suburban cookie-cutter South Asian married couples have their own special, dirty, scandalous deviances they will never reveal. I think I would like Azar's friends' wives more if they cried about their husbands' infidelities rather than talked about a bake sale for some charity they couldn't care less about. But us wives are all just for show anyway.

Azar turns down his music as he pulls into Simi's driveway. Her lawn is as perfectly trimmed as a military haircut. I bet she forced Ikram to mow it this morning because she knew I was coming.

"All right baby, charge the cab to my card after you're done brunch. I'll see you at home. I'm going to be really late again tonight so just have dinner without me."

Azar casually unlocks my door and leans in for a goodbye kiss.

For some reason, Linda's picture flashes into my mind, and I refuse to kiss him. "You're going to be late again? Why?"

"Don't start, Nisha. You know I have work. What else do I do but work?" Looking irritated, he turns away from me.

"You never even talk about whatever it is you're working so hard on."

"You wouldn't even understand if I tried to explain it. It's complicated software stuff—a lot more complicated than the science of contouring a nose. There's a lot of technical terms and business procedures you know nothing about."

"Why don't you try me?" I try to catch his eye, but he won't look at me.

"I'm not going to do this with you now. I'm going to be late." He looks at his watch, which is a signal for me to leave. "Go do some shopping, get your nails done, and order yourself a nice, big steak. Don't burden yourself with things you wouldn't understand."

"I'm trying to understand. I'm trying to know every part of you. We are going to have a baby together."

"I know we are and that's why I'm working so hard—strollers, nannies, and trips to Disney World don't come for free, Nisha."

I pretend to calm down. Of course, he is right, those things don't come for free and without him, I'd be in no position to ever attain them.

"I work for us, Nisha."

My anger suddenly evaporates along with the image of Linda and her shiny, bright hair, when I realize we're parked right in front of Simi's door. We kiss and hug each other goodbye. Somebody is watching.

Simi waddles around her kitchen with one hand cradling the bottom of her jutting belly. She's crammed herself into a light, polka-dot blouse and grey sweatpants; her oily dark hair sits in a messy bun on top of her head. She's five months pregnant and looks every bit of it. She was never slim but the baby growing inside her has made her once Rubenesque figure explode.

She has a plain face with thin lips, an average nose with a broad tip, low cheekbones, and a fleshy chin. There may have been a decent oval-shaped visage there once upon a time, but I haven't seen it in the five years that I've known her through Ikram. However, I have always liked her eyes and her smile. Her warm brown eyes are large and round like a curious child's. Her smile reveals two deep and perfectly symmetrical dimples which add to her unique girlish charm.

I watch her body secretively whenever she sways away from me. I am petrified. As much as I want to give my husband and our mothers a little bundle of joy, I'd like to keep my skinny body the way it is. My body is the only good thing I ever gave Azar. I work hard at it and its appearance is nothing short of an accomplishment. It's my only accomplishment in life.

I dare not admit this to Simi because she will only point out how the miracle of a baby trumps some measly weight gain. She is too blinded by her own halo to see how much a woman's body and appearance shapes her entire life. Had my waist not been tiny and my jawline not defined, a man like Azar would never have looked at me. And if I don't lose weight right after giving birth, Azar's eyes will wander and women like Linda will star in his fantasies.

"How are you two feeling?" I smile at Simi's belly.

"Well, one of us is happy and kicking and the other isn't sleeping," Simi says, pointing to her puffy eyes as she cracks the predictable joke, "This kid kicks so much, we're sure he's going to be a soccer player."

I force out a laugh and now we smile at each other with no idea what to say next. Simi and I don't have much in common. She's a social butterfly who hosts or attends fundraisers weekly, to save the trees or feed the poor, or something else and everybody on her social media circuits know about it. I'm a voluntary hermit who doesn't care to save anybody because I know everything's going to hell anyway. All I ever post of my life is

my perfect marriage, my perfect vacations, my expensive outfits, and my expensive dinners.

"So?" Simi turns away from the oven and looks at me imp-
ishly. "Any luck for you and Azar yet?"

"No, not yet, but we are definitely trying."

"Oh, don't stress about it. It'll happen for you when God
decides it's time."

I'm not at all stressed about it. Becoming pregnant and
having a baby is something I'm pursuing to pass the time. I've
never felt giddy over miniature baby clothes or considered
our friends' screeching and drooling brats as anything near a
miracle.

Indeed, nobody is a miracle. We are all here because of two
people's lust, boredom, irresponsibility, desperate need to
cement their relationship, egoistic desire to replicate themselves, selfish retirement plans, or cultural expectations. I'm
not desperate to become a mother; it's just something that I
must do because I am who I am from the place I'm from.

Simi stretches her back straight and sighs with discomfort
as she stirs the deliciously fragrant curry cooking on her stove.
Open jars of spices and cut vegetables are scattered all over her
kitchen countertop. I'm confused as to why she's standing heavily pregnant in the kitchen and cooking curry from scratch when
her banker husband, Ikram, can very easily afford to hire a chef.

"Do you want me to help you with anything? Should we just
order some delivery?"

"Oh, Ikram and I have decided I'm not going to eat outside
food while I'm pregnant." Simi looks at me over her shoulder
and warns, "You just don't know what's in restaurant food. It
could harm the baby."

"So you haven't had any restaurant food the last five
months?"

"My mother-in-law has been so amazing, cooking for me. She asks me to say what I want and she makes it fresh."

Simi seems to have forgotten that she posts pictures of every fancy meal she eats at restaurants and I can easily prove she has eaten outside at least twice a week since becoming pregnant. As for her mother-in-law, it's common knowledge in the community that she's always thought of Simi as too social and too outspoken for her son. I strongly doubt her traditional mother-in-law, who fervently opposed her marriage to Ikram, is suddenly at her beck and call.

"You are so lucky to have a mother-in-law like that," I tell her, "and not eating outside is a great call. They put pesticides in everything these days and the salt and fat content is just ridiculous."

Simi smiles and tells me what I want to hear, "Well, you will never have to worry about fat content when you get pregnant, inshallah—skinny women like you burn the weight off so fast."

"Thank you."

Most of my encounters with Azar's friends' wives are just long exchanges of ego-stroking. We don't want any tension or any conflict. But we all probably hate each other.

"So how's your makeup business going?" Simi pours me a cup of tea. "How much sugar?"

"It's not too busy and no sugar please."

Before handing me the teacup, she asks, "Do you want any Red Powder in your cup?"

I suddenly awake with excitement. "You guys have it in your house?"

"Yes, of course we do. You sound shocked?"

"No, I just thought you wouldn't have it because you're pregnant."

"We always have it available just in case guests want it. I

miss having it in my tea, that's for sure. Did you want some?"

"Yes." I answer without a second thought. "Yes, please."

Simi mixes the Red Powder into my tea and hands me my cup and a plate of biscuits. She looks longingly at the jar where she keeps the herb before putting it back into the cupboard. She pours herself some orange juice and awkwardly manages to thrust her heavy body onto the stool across from me.

"You look like you really want a sip of this. Are you getting a little antsy about the delivery?"

"Oh no, I don't waste time worrying about that—the baby has to come out," she laughs. "I'm just a little worried about the Annual Gala."

Simi is on the board of the SAPAG, the South Asian Professionals Annual Gala, along with a bunch of other house-wives like her who are not professionals at all. They throw a great party though. Every year the venue and decoration seem to be fancier, the celebrity guest speaker more famous. The five-hundred-dollar tickets are priced to make sure the party is exclusive and inaccessible to those who can't afford to shell out that amount to charity.

Showing off moral superiority is the foremost reason why people attend the SAPAG. The gala is the simplest way to show they really care about the less fortunate: they just have to buy a tax-deductible ticket, nod to whatever the speakers utter, applaud some presentation with pictures of starving children, and then they're free to eat and dance the night away.

"Oh my God, I'm sure you guys are going to make it bigger and better than ever," I tell her. "What is the cause this year?"

"Women," Simi announces proudly. "This year is all about girls and women. We are splitting the money three-ways and giving to several girls' schools in Bangladesh, a widows' charity in India, and a women's hospital in Pakistan."

"That's amazing. You're helping so many of the less fortunate. I think you guys make a true difference."

Not much, though. Women's issues in South Asia can never be solved with a little gifted money, though extra cash is always nice, and perhaps at least one young girl in a village will graduate high school—but no amount of money can help her avoid an arranged marriage after.

"It's going to be great, we have so many corporate sponsors this year and several TV channels have shown an interest, and the guest speaker is just incredible and—" She suddenly stops, takes a deep breath, and places a shaky hand on her belly.

"Are you all right? Are you going into labour?"

"No, no." She laughs nervously before she buries her face in her palms. "I'm just so overwhelmed, Nisha. There is so much to do and this baby is slowing me down."

The Red Powder begins to take me over now and suddenly, I sort of like her.

"Do you need help, Simi?"

Her normally satisfied face reappears. "Would you help me? Would you please help me with the Annual Gala this year?"

"Who, me?" I look over my shoulder instinctively, in case there's somebody else she's talking to.

"Yes, would you help me with the gala, Nisha? Please?"

"I-I-I've never really planned an event of that type before— I mean, I have no experience at all," I laugh. "But I'd love to book you a relaxing massage or manicure or something to help relieve your stress. I can give you a makeover?"

I don't know whether to be shocked or flattered that Simi would trust me to help her with one of the community's most prestigious events of the year. This is not some baby shower or a Ramadan dinner; this is a fundraiser that's sponsored by prominent businesses and written about in the newspapers. I wouldn't trust me to be the doorman.

"Please, Nisha? I need as many volunteers as possible. You'd be volunteering for a really good cause."

"B-but I thought you already have enough people. There's like ten of you guys on the board, no?"

Simi drops her polite façade, slams her glass down and huffs, "Everybody's fucking pregnant."

I never thought the f-word would ever escape Simi's pristine mouth and I'm thoroughly impressed.

"We only have about three months to put this thing together, and every time I need something done somebody always has an ultrasound or a goddamn visit from their midwife!" Simi sighs with annoyance. "I'm sorry I'm swearing so much. This is really stressing me out."

"I can see that. Maybe you should just take a deep breath," I sip my Red Powder with not a single care in the world. "I'm sure everybody will pull through eventually."

"Just in case they don't . . . can I count on you to help out this year? I mean, unless you're busy with something other than the makeup?"

"Well, I have to do my workouts, you know. Four days of cardio, three days of weights. And Azar likes all of his meals made fresh. And I have to keep the house clean—you know how many hours that takes."

"Please, Nisha? You just have to come to our meetings, help with some phone calls and maybe a little bit of driving to pick up stuff? That's all."

That doesn't sound too challenging. I don't know if it's the Red Powder making me pliable or the desperate look in Simi's eyes, but I suddenly agree to offer my help.

"Sure, I'll gladly come on board," I shrug. "It is for a good cause."

This might be a nice way to pass the hours and impress Azar. He always tells me to get a hobby and maybe this will show him a new side of me; I'll show him I'm good for something more than just contouring a nose.

Simi nearly jumps out of her chair and embraces me in a way I haven't been embraced in a long time. This is a genuine hug and I can feel her gratitude. I feel my respect for her blooming until she suddenly shoves her phone into my face.

"Let's take a selfie so I can announce that you're on board!"

Before I can object, Simi flashes a big smile with her arm around me and takes our picture. She swiftly removes her arm and posts the picture for all to see. I do hope Azar sees her post as soon as possible.

"Thank you so much, Nisha! The other members will be thrilled to have you helping us. I'll make sure your name goes on the pamphlets and you get credit. You might even be lucky enough to talk to the guest speaker backstage!"

"Who's the guest speaker this year?"

"It's the most famous and inspirational person we've ever had in the gala yet," Simi gloats. "The one and only Amatullah!"

"Amatullah? That name sounds familiar. What's her last name?"

Simi bobs up and down with laughter. "She doesn't need a last name, she's Amatullah. You seriously don't know who she is?"

I blush. "Well, the name sounds very familiar."

"Internationally famous best-selling author? Mentor to celebrities? Award-winning lecturer? The face of charities on three different continents? Songwriter, poet, leading activist for women's rights?"

I blush and lie to cover my embarrassment, "Oh, that Amatullah? Yes, the name sure sounded familiar."

"Have you read any of her books?"

"I skimmed through some, but never really finished any."

"You have to read her books!" Simi appears outraged. "They're incredible. I have all of them; I can lend you some today."

"No, no, I'll buy them. I'll read a few soon," I promise, knowing quite well that I won't.

I don't read books anymore. I used to inhale them as a child, when thinking and expanding the corners of my mind excited me. These days, I watch reality TV shows: cheap and quick entertainment for stagnating souls.

"Please do read some of Amatullah's material before the gala," Simi pleads. "You don't want to appear clueless if you're lucky enough to talk to her. Some people pay thousands for the chance to just watch her speak for thirty minutes."

"Well," I sip the last of my tea, "this Amatullah must have a lot of interesting things to say then."

5

AZAR WAS SO IMPRESSED by my agreeing to help Simi with the Annual Gala that he promised he'd be home on time this upcoming Friday and take me out to dinner. I'll need something new and nice to wear for our date, of course, and so I'm spending a muggy weekday morning roaming inside a cold, air-conditioned mall.

I haven't found an outfit I liked yet, but I've bought scented candles, a cute pair of feather earrings, a keychain with an adorable panda bear ornament, another shade of nude lipstick, and eyebrow gel. I've been strolling around from one end of the mall to another, looking to throw cash on dumb things that look great under the bright store lights. Shopping feels almost as good as being high on the Red Powder: they both numb and distract me, help me fill the long hours of the day.

I'm indulging both my vices today. I put five teaspoons of the Red Powder in my tea this morning—one spoonful more than my usual four because I need a bit of courage today. I have Linda's number written down and I want to call her. I want to hear her voice.

Azar came home late last night and hardly spoke to me

because, apparently, he was tired. I decided to go into his phone when he was sleeping and found a message from Linda again. I read it this time and found nothing particularly disturbing about it: she was asking about some files and if he wanted to see them. The part that bothered me was why she needed that question answered at midnight.

It's almost noon now and I figure Azar and his team should be out for lunch. I don't know what I expect to find out by calling Linda. Maybe I'll hear Azar's voice in the background. Maybe she won't even pick up. Maybe she will have a deep, unattractive manlike voice and I can finally breathe in peace again.

Unless Azar finds a deep voice in a woman sexy. I don't know if I even know what he truly finds sexy anymore. I always thought I'd be enough. I was working hard enough to be enough.

"Can I have a large iced caramel latte, please?" I ask a bouncy young man behind the café counter.

I take a greedy sip of my delicious, creamy coffee and find a seat in an isolated corner of the food court. I dial Linda's number with absolutely no idea what to say. One part of me just wants to ask her directly: are you seeing my husband after work? Another part of me, as I press the call button, just wants to pretend like she doesn't exist. Then maybe my nagging feelings will just stop.

"*Hello?*" A high-pitched, girly voice answers the phone. "*Hi?*" She does indeed exist, and her voice is sexy.

"*Hello?*" She asks impatiently and I can tell she's quite young.

I breathe into the line, speechless. I don't hear anything in the background. I decide to hang up.

Linda sounds just the way she looks in her picture on his phone: young, attractive, approachable. There's no way she wouldn't get Azar's attention or any other man's. Even if there's nothing going on between them, Azar has noticed her enough to allow her to text him at any time. He has thought of her. This mysterious girl has been running through my husband's mind—maybe even when his hands were on my skin.

I put my phone away and breathe deeply. The Red Powder is helping me feel the floor beneath my feet and stay focused on whatever's before my eyes and not the storm brewing in my head. I watch all the strange and new faces at the food court, follow their lips as they eat their burgers and fries. I see a large group of very old men sitting around a table, their canes and walkers parked beside them as they chat and chuckle. They make me smile.

There aren't many people in the mall at this hour except retirees and new mothers. Unlike the old men who look more like hooting youngsters in their cliques, the mothers all sit quiet and alone beside their strollers, accompanied by their sleeping babies. Some look serene, but I pay attention to the young women with bags under their eyes, who haven't had time to pay much attention to themselves. There's a look of defeat in some eyes; one I remember so vividly that it feels like I've travelled back in time.

I remember how my mother looked when Tariq and I were growing up. She knew she couldn't stop time; she knew the world went on every day without her while she was locked up at home, feeding us, washing dishes and clothes, cooking. By giving us our lives, she had forfeited hers. She never once said she regretted us, or that she wished she could step out of the house, or that she was downright miserable—but her eyes always signaled what her mouth was too ashamed to say.

I watch the laughing group of old men next to the new mothers who scroll through their cellphones drearily and I wonder if it's they who are closer to death. They all remind me of my mother, and I imagine they died the day their babies were born. There is no time now to recount the stories of their lives, no time to shed tears or heal, no time to build on a legacy that doesn't include their loin fruit—the baby needs milk, a diaper change, rocking, attention, a doctor's visit, or something else that requires their time and energy. These women are the walking dead.

But their husbands are somewhere, alive. Just like Azar, who's in a downtown patio right now eating a scrumptious bruschetta with his coworkers and checking out the tanned women who pass by in their low-cut summer dresses. Nobody raises an eyebrow if they spend all day outside of the home, away from their kids—just like my father did—if they play the honoured part of a provider. They are still visible in society and their stories continue; their baby is just a chapter in their book, not the closing paragraph.

Am I ready to die for Azar? I have barely lived yet. Most of my adult life has been spent replaying the past in my head and trying things to run away from it. A baby won't allow me to run away from anything—I'll be stuck in the house dying slowly, forever haunted by the images, the injustice, the knowledge of Riad and Sonia being somewhere happy and thriving. Everything they did to me will be buried along with me.

Nobody will ever know just how angry I am . . . except my own innocent child.

I'm suddenly stunned by a rare moment of clarity: I can't be a mother. Not now. Not yet. I must tell Azar as soon as possible. I must tell him tonight.

A crying baby interrupts my trance and I watch on as its mother tries to rock it back to calmness. Her cheeks flush as she smiles embarrassedly at another mother sitting nearby, as if it's her fault the baby is crying.

"I think someone's a hungry bear," the other mother laughs, offering an unsolicited opinion.

The red-faced mother nods in agreement as she puts the shrieking baby back into the stroller briefly while collecting the remains of her lunch and throwing it into the garbage bin behind her. I watch on as she rushes towards the washrooms, pushing the stroller along with one arm while cradling the baby with the other.

Azar is propped up on his pillow as he points eagerly to the nightstand on my side of the bed. Freshly showered and shirtless under the duvets, he calls me with his eyes. For a second, I believe he wants me again and I'm sweetly reminded of the earliest months of our marriage. He used to bring a bottle of wine and a box of chocolates to our bedroom on the weekends. He didn't make any comments on how many calories I ate back then. He'd feed me the chocolates one by one, tease me with the wine glass, and whisper sweet nothings in my ear all night until we fell asleep with a throbbing sugar headache. I used to think, in those short-lived months, that he would always spoil me with such care and attention.

Watching my husband relaxed on the bed while I'm battling the picture and voice of Linda in my head, I begin to approach him like a loyal and forgiving puppy. I just do as Azar says without thinking twice about it; it has become a bad habit. I see the gift on the nightstand is ovulation strips and a plastic cup for me to pee in. Now my anger turns into repugnance, and I find myself standing still before him in my nightgown, ruminating in the dim light.

I know the words must be said, but I don't know which ones and in which order. I can't bring a child into our lives right now. I don't want a child before I get some type of justice for what happened to me. I need peace. Azar won't understand any of my reasoning unless I tell him all about my childhood. And I won't do that.

"Is everything okay? What are you thinking about?"

"I-I need to talk to you about something," I stutter and look down at my hands, afraid to lock eyes with him.

"Yes?" he asks me impatiently.

"M-maybe we should wait."

"Wait?" He turns and scowls at me, like a teacher ready to scold an impossible student. "Wait for what?"

"To have kids. I think we should wait. There's really no need to rush, don't you agree?"

"There's really no need to slow down either, Nisha. Are you getting any younger?"

"No."

"You know every year you get older, you have fewer eggs left and the ones that remain aren't as good as the ones you had. That's high school biology, Nisha."

"Yes, I knew that."

"Well, do you want our kids to be different than the other kids at school? Do you want them to be bullied because they're dumber? Or because they look different? All because you were too selfish to have them at a responsible age?"

"Of course not, but I just think we shouldn't rush it." I sit on my side of the bed and turn to face him. "You know I have all these issues in my head to sort out—I think I should sort them out before becoming a mother. Taking care of a little person is not some small thing, Azar."

"No worries, you'll have nine months to enjoy all the therapy sessions you want before you actually do become a mother," Azar smiles dismissively and scoots over to my side.

He places my hand in his and plants a reassuring kiss on my

palm. "I'll be here for you. I am here for you. I know change and not knowing the future can be scary, but we are doing it together. It's not like you're going to raise the baby all on your own."

Yeah, and where will you be? I think to myself, *With your office whore?*

I hate that I can no longer control the doubt and the anger. Linda has nested herself in my thoughts, in my bedroom. A new version of myself has been born and I hate her. I don't want to be a suspicious and bitter wife, always making sly comments to herself when her husband speaks. I want to be the unquestioning and docile woman on Azar's arms again, the smiling one who swallows her pride, her emotions, and her desires and lets the natural process of her unfeeling stomach dispose of it all. It may not always be the tastiest option to be an obedient wife, but it sure is the healthiest. I know, through an entire childhood of witnessing my loud and nagging mother, that keeping your mouth shut and looking the other way is how to keep the peace in a marriage.

I take the first step towards peace. I recognize and respect that Azar is always deaf to my protests no matter how loud I scream, so I give up on this conversation. I'm all right now. I take his gift and disappear to the en suite. I finish the degrading process and balk at the positive result.

"It's a go," I announce as I return to Azar with a forced smile upon my face, praying inwardly with all my might that I don't fall pregnant.

Azar's disinterested gaze now turns seductive as he invites me to lie next to him. I take my nightdress off and hang it on the bedpost. I'd made the mistake once to drop it on the floor and the result was Azar angrily telling me the floor was dirty as I stood there naked for him. I take my bra and panties off, fold them, and stack them away on the chair by Azar's closet. I stand naked before the mirror on the vanity as I search my drawer full of perfumes for Azar's favourite.

I see my reflection in the mirror—the voluptuous actress with her long black hair loose over her glowing shoulders—and give myself a quiet pep talk. The truth is I'm not in the mood to be touched by Azar and to be surrounded by his scent. It's not just the stress of Linda or the fear of becoming a mother; it's the nothingness of it all. What once used to feel intimate now feels clinical. There is nothing sensual about us making love anymore; it's just cold hard science, a biological procedure where the expression of love and the need for touch is just an afterthought.

I can feel Azar's eyes watching my nudity and as soon as I've accepted what will happen next, the journey begins. This journey is not triggered by the Red Powder but it's just as uncontrollable as those drug-fuelled episodes. I escape my mind—or my mind escapes me—as I recoil with a mix of emotions. My mind simply won't allow me to be here and forces me to think about something, anything, that saves me from the truth of being intimate.

I can't separate the truth of being here in this moment with my husband and being in the past with Riad. He was my first sexual experience, and I spent all our times together denying reality. I—whether it was my soul or my brain—couldn't allow him to do the things he did and so I left. I left my body behind to be abused and flew away to another place. I did it so many times and with so much concentration, that that's the sexual being I became permanently. No matter how pleasurable and no matter how desired, I'm never here when my body is bare. In five years, I've never had an orgasm with my husband that I haven't faked.

Azar kisses me and I kiss him back with a mechanical tongue. He touches my shoulders, the back of my thighs, my waist; I feel his hands all over me, but his touch is dull and trivial. Clothing is what I think about as we descend onto the bed and I feel his weight over me. Yes, clothing. Dresses. Beautiful dresses. Silky sarees. Floral summer skirts that go well with a white blouse.

He pushes himself into me and I'm thinking about the Annual Gala and what I'll be wearing. I feel him thrusting and moaning under his breath and I see myself in something sparkly red this year. I sing the song that awakens his ego—a "yes" here and a "oh my god" there—as I decide on a lehenga over a saree. I see myself entering the hall, hair half up and half down with a glittery headpiece, catching everybody's attention with my dazzling outfit and jewellery.

Azar finishes and I descend back into the present, completely unaware of how much time has passed. He rolls off me, stares at the ceiling, and makes a comment about how great it was.

"Amazing," I whisper as I cover myself immediately with the duvet.

"God, let it be a boy!" Azar laughs as he turns off his lamp and turns over to sleep.

I keep my lamp on and stare at the shadows on the ceiling. I wait to be mobile again—for my soul and brain to tell my body that what just happened was acceptable. I erase the memory and wait for Riad's face to leave my restless mind.

6

WE SIT LIKE DIGNIFIED diplomats around a coffee table, our postures perfect and smiles plastered on our nodding, agreeable faces. Everybody drinks their tea with their pinky fingers daintily pointed away from their cups, chatting away about pregnancies, babies, newly discovered recipes, and the loveable blunders of their otherwise perfect husbands. I turn my head mindlessly towards whoever speaks the loudest while I wonder who had sex last night and if they faked it as well as they're faking everything right now.

I've had a throbbing headache since the beginning of this rainy day, yet Azar called me a cab and forced me to join this meeting. He said working on the Annual Gala would be the most prestigious opportunity I'd ever get. And If I did a good job, they might ask me to be on the board every year, and I'd finally have something to do. I think Azar just wants me out of the house.

He wouldn't allow me to sprinkle the Red Powder in my tea this morning, worried that I'd act strange and embarrass myself in front of his friends' wives. I promised him I wouldn't drink it today and reluctantly declined when I was offered it.

All the planners of the Annual Gala are present, six of them here in Mariam's living room and two others by webcam. Mariam, along with Simi, Divya, and Jasleen are all pregnant. Tanzila has a one-year-old and Priya gave birth just months ago. They both seem ecstatic about leaving their babies with their mothers for the afternoon. The two wives on webcam, Rabia and Shanaz, don't have mothers who live in the city and refused to leave their babies with their in-laws.

"I feel like I'm committing a crime," Priya laughs and the others follow. "I'm so used to having a baby on me. I feel like I should be rocking something right now."

"Once they're here, you're never without them," Tanzila warns the pregnant women. "Trust me, if you have something to do, do it now."

"Well, I would if I could move!" Divya, who just entered her last trimester, half-jokes to a concurring Simi and Jasleen.

Mariam is in her kitchen preparing all sorts of desserts and snack platters. The coffee table is already covered with bagels and croissants that will be end up in the trash. The endless barrage of food aesthetically arranged on gilded plates and wooden planks is just content for the women's social media. Everybody should know that we, the special chosen housewives, are planning this important event while munching on a lavish feast. We have it so good.

Mariam, who announced her pregnancy recently, shuffles into the living room with another spectacular tray and announces, "Last call for tea before we begin the planning, guys!"

She places the large, circular plate in the middle of the table, and everybody helps to remove the surrounding napkins, crumbs, and whatever else makes a food table realistic. The women excitedly stand up with their cellphones in hand and snap away.

"Oh my God, where did you order these macarons from?"

"Did you make these muffins yourself?"

"The sprinkled donuts add a really fun touch!"

I stand up and quickly take a picture because I don't want to be weird, and the beautiful platter is indeed colourful enough to be picture-worthy. However, I can't force myself to gush over the positioning of pink donuts and green grapes as if it's some type of art exhibit. Only a truly stupid person would do that and, ironically, I am the stupidest person here.

There are two engineering degrees, three arts degrees, two MBAs, and one MD in this room. Eight careers abandoned to find excitement in the beauty of fluffy cupcakes.

Besides having the tightest waist in a room full of pregnant women, I have no accolades. I have no degree or training in anything important, no impressive resume, no interesting stories of volunteering in some exotic village, no great deed, no legacy at all. Unlike these women, I am a potato who deserves to be exiled to the domestic wasteland, whipped by the slaveholder I call *husband*, forced to change diapers and make chai until my wrinkly hands succumb to arthritis.

These women all had something great they happily tossed away to tend to their wombs. Sure, they are heroes on Mother's Day and all year round in greeting cards, but they leave no impression on anybody except their own offspring and maybe their mothers-in-law.

I refuse to believe they are as happy as they let on. No, they must be wearing a mask just like me.

After we all help ourselves to some sweets, Simi leads us with a quick, "So the hall has been booked but do we all agree not to use their caterers? I think the caterers last year were perfectly fine—I called some of them and they've already saved the date. They're literally just waiting for us to confirm and give them a deposit."

Jasleen, who appears to enjoy arguing for the sake of conversation, wrinkles her nose. "I was not a huge fan of the appetizers last year—far too oily."

"Samosas are supposed to be oily," Divya, who clearly wants to get out of here, quickly, says. "Who wants a dry samosa?"

"Well, actually," Rabia chimes in from Mariam's laptop, "I feel like us South Asians are becoming more aware of eating too much oil and it might be an issue."

"Yes, Zayd won't even let me cook using anything but margarine anymore!" Tanzila finishes her donut before adding, "We don't want to appear like we are encouraging unhealthy eating."

"What about little whole-grain sandwiches filled with different salads like tuna and crab? Or little bagels filled with cream cheese and lox? And we can put, like, vegetable and fruit platters right next to it?" Mariam says, showing off her culinary creativity.

"This is the Annual South Asian Gala and there's nothing South Asian about bagels and lox," Jasleen says and shakes her head in strong disagreement.

My headache worsens as the conversation heats up. The wives on the committee all want their own ideas realized but won't risk appearing loud and unladylike. The result is a back-and-forth exchange of covert attacks on each others' intelligence wrapped up in polite language and delivered with a sweet tone. There is no end in sight.

I finish a few macarons when my stomach begins to bloat and rumble violently. The pain intensifies and now I feel dizzy. Not wanting to interrupt the lively conversation, I continue to sit quietly and hide my sudden pain.

"What do you think, Nisha?" Tanzila suddenly asks me and the bickering stops.

"What do I think about what?"

"The appetizers?" Simi smiles. "Do you think we should keep it deep-fried or get something more Canadian this year?"

"I think samosas are fine," I shrug as I hug my stomach in pain. "Maybe you can have both deep-fried snacks and a variety of fresh salad bowls and the guests can choose if they want to eat healthy or not."

With great enthusiasm, they all agree with me—not because they like me but because they know I'm only on the committee this year and so I pose no threat. A fool unites just as well as an enemy.

"Well, our current caterer doesn't offer fresh fruit platters, unfortunately," Simi pouts. "Who wants to shop around for a vendor who can do both fruit and deep-fried appetizers? It has to be done by the end of this week."

"Why don't you do it, Nisha? It was your idea, after all," Jasleen says.

The other women look reluctant relinquishing control, but then know how tired they are with their pregnancies and kids. And so they all encourage me to take on my first task as an event planner.

"Sure." I accept the challenge.

"I actually have a ton of business cards right here," Simi rummages through the pile of folders on her lap. "All we need from you is to find out who serves what and if they're available on our day and give us a list."

"You don't want me to book—"

"No, no!" Tanzila doesn't let me finish my sentence. "Just compile a list and give it to me or Mariam."

"Yes, Mariam always tastes the food," Divya says and brilliantly adds a veiled insult, "Tanzila does all the haggling because she's the best at counting every dollar."

Tanzila thinks of something smart to say but I quickly speak before she can, because I'm too dizzy to take any more headache-inducing arguing. "All right, I'll only make the phone calls and nothing else."

I stand up to grab the business cards from Simi but a sudden bout of dizziness forces me right back down. The room seems to be spinning around and I grab the armrest of the sofa to balance myself.

"What's wrong?" The women rise up from their chairs and come up to me.

"Are you okay, Nisha?" Divya grabs my shoulder.

". . . just feeling dizzy," I mumble and rub my forehead.

"Do you feel nauseous?" Simi asks.

"Oh my God, she's pregnant!" An ecstatic Shanaz squeals through the webcam. "Yay!"

Before I can suggest a less scary explanation, a frenzy of excited shrieks pierces through my ears. The women hug and congratulate me, celebrating my possible induction into new motherhood.

"Finally, you'll be one of us, Nisha!"

I try to convince them and myself, "I haven't had enough tea today—it's probably just caffeine withdrawal."

The women throw their heads back and laugh at my explanation. They tell me not to worry, this will be the greatest journey of my life, which is exactly what I fear. This great journey might be the end of all greater journeys.

"You should call Azar," Simi finds my cellphone on the coffee table and hands it to me. "I'll give you a ride home and stay with you until he comes. You can join our next meeting."

Smiling, they all retreat to their seats and quietly continue to discuss the gala as I call Azar.

"*Hello?*" Azar answers with disdain in his voice, annoyed that

I'm calling him at work.

"Hey, I'm still at Mariam's, but I'm not feeling too well," I say as quietly as possible, not wanting to attract the women's attention to my conversation.

"*Is this about your depression again?*" he barks. "*Nisha, do you understand that I'm at work?*"

"No, I'm feeling dizzy. Like, very dizzy. And bloated. I have a headache so bad I feel like I'm going to die."

"*That's great news!*"

Azar quickly changes his tone, and I don't need to see him to know he's beaming.

"Let's not get too excited; it could just be withdrawal from you-know-what," I whisper and mumble incoherently on purpose.

These women can never know that I drink teaspoons of the Red Powder almost daily. If they find out, they'll commend me for being a fun-loving rebel to my face while happily telling everybody I'm a drug addict behind my back.

"*Why don't you get one of the girls to drive you home right now and then you can take Victoria to the drugstore to get a pregnancy test?*"

"You'll make me drive Victoria?" I ask, baffled. "By myself?"

"*You'll have to. I'm sorry, baby, but I'm going to be home really late tonight. There's a ton of work.*"

I'm angry at Azar for leaving me stranded tonight of all nights. For him the pregnancy test, negative or positive, is my business only—just a casual snippet of news to discuss over tomorrow's breakfast. I want to shout at him at the top of my lungs but there are eight pairs of hawk eyes secretly watching this interaction between a perfect couple.

"Ok, honey," I swallow my pride as always and hope nobody heard the heavy gulp. "I will see you at home."

"*Call me as soon as you find out the result!*"

I hang up abruptly and lie to Simi about Azar already being home and waiting for me. Simi wastes no time and finds her car keys while I say goodbye to everybody. They all hug me and tell me to update them, to which I nod enthusiastically. I know I most certainly won't.

"Who's Victoria, by the way?" Tanzila casually asks as I'm walking away, apparently having listened to my phone conversation.

"Victoria is Azar's early midlife-crisis fancy sportscar," I reply lightly with a laugh. The ridiculously expensive hunk of metal sits in our garage most of the year.

The women all giggle with amusement and Simi says, "Azar is so funny. You're lucky to have him."

The violent drumming of rain on the pavement outside is daunting. After a brief pause, I make a dash to the car and get behind Victoria's steering wheel. The sleek leather seat warms my butt as I place a large thermos filled to the brim with chai and a heavy dose of the Red Powder in the cupholder. The engine roars, I have a generous sip of tea, and I feel a strange sense of freedom.

Tonight could be the last night I enjoy the company of the Red Powder, and so I'm treating myself to six teaspoons of it. I feel as if I'm saying goodbye to a secret lover, bittersweetly giving him one last kiss. Of course, possibly being pregnant, I feel guilty for drinking my last cup right now, but I need it for the ache that's imbued in every corner of my body. Living with pain can't possibly be good for the baby either.

After years of reflexively crossing my legs in the passenger seat, it's intimidating being in the driver's seat. I'd be smart to wait and get the pregnancy test done after the storm, but I can't tame the maddening curiosity about whether there is a pea-sized human being floating around inside me or not.

I pull out of the garage. In the blinding rain and the darkness of the late evening, and with my nausea, it's a challenge to keep all my attention on the road in front of me. With vivid thoughts of rocking a rosy-cheeked, raven-haired cherub in my arms, I drive straight through a neighbourhood stop sign and splash a poor old lady by the bus stand.

I swear at myself.

Suddenly the traffic around me appears to slow down. The Red Powder kicks in quickly and powerfully and I feel the familiar sense of calm and exhale with gratitude. The streetlights are twinkling like brightly coloured stars and I can hear the rain dancing on the road. The world is beautiful again.

The rain escalates into a violent downpour. It hits my car in pellets. I can see clearly in front only for a split second before another flood washes down the windshield, blurring my vision of the dark, empty road ahead. I'm driving blindly now, wildly guessing what street I'm on. I'm inside a horror movie, but I'm not afraid at all. All I notice are the scenic flashes of whatever my headlights illuminate in the blackness.

As I turn into what I believe is the strip mall with the drugstore, I realize I've turned into a completely unfamiliar street. If I wasn't being hugged by the soothing and reassuring arms of the Red Powder, fear and panic would terrorize me, because I cannot find a single recognizable landmark. Whatever street this is, it feels abandoned. I decide I should pull over and turn on the GPS on my phone when suddenly the rain slows down as quickly as it started.

"I'm not afraid," I promise myself in an uplifting sing-song voice. "I'm not afraid at all."

A smile creeps on my face and I begin to laugh. I don't know why I find being lost in the dark so funny—I know it isn't funny,

I know it should be downright frightening—but I can't seem to control my laughter. I haven't laughed like this since I was a little kid: my mouth shamelessly open and my eyes scrunched up uncontrollably despite the Botox restraining my face. The Red Powder has never taken me this high off the ground before. Up here, somewhere miles away from reality, I feel truly happy.

Through the gentle drizzle now, I see a bright red light on the horizon. I can't believe my luck when I see PHARMACY spelled out next to the bowl of Hygeia. What are the chances of effortlessly ending up exactly where I needed to be after being completely lost?

"Thank you, God!"

I quit laughing, gather myself, and make my way to the inviting red sign. There's nothing around the brightly lit store except a wall of tall trees behind it and a small empty parking lot in front. I'm unable to see what's behind the trees as I drive down a winding road that descends to the parking lot. I think to myself that this is a rather odd place for a small pharmacy—a gas station would've fared much better in a place with no houses or apartment buildings or signs of life anywhere.

I feel like the last woman on earth as I park and dart towards the pharmacy with my wallet in my hand, raindrops still falling. I don't see anybody inside and I'm glad about this because I'd be embarrassed to pay for a pregnancy test in front of a line of people, inviting them to imagine me peeing on a stick.

As I step inside, a coldness disturbs my carefree mood. It's far too early for the Red Powder to wear off—I sure hope it doesn't wear off until I'm safe in my bed because I know the drop from this height will be disastrous. I must be pregnant. That's the only explanation. This must be one of the strange things that happen during pregnancy. I'm cold because I'm probably losing blood. This parasite baby must be stealing my blood.

The frigid store, with its peculiar checkered floor and red shelves, is so quiet that I can hear.myself breathing. There is no cheesy music playing on the intercom and there are no customers or workers in sight. I figure the cashier must be some irresponsible teenager video-chatting with his friends in the backroom. I cross my arms and rub my shoulders for some warmth as I search for the aisle displaying pregnancy tests.

None of the aisles in this bizarre drugstore is labelled except the one furthest away from the entrance. On top of that aisle hangs a bright sign with marquee lights—something I most definitely have never seen in a pharmacy before. The sign reads the awkward words: YOUR CHOICE.

Out of sheer curiosity, I walk towards that aisle to see what on earth it's stacking. Through the shelves I peek at the other aisles, looking for a worker. I find and walk past the pregnancy tests, thinking I'll grab one on the way out. They're hung up like omens right next to the condoms and the lubricants, a visual reminder of where the fun ends.

I turn into the aisle that will supposedly give me a choice and see nothing but hundreds of coloured drug bottles. There are no labels on any of these bottles and no price tags under them, but they appear to be organized by the colours of the rainbow. The bottles near me are different shades of red and the bottles at the further end appear to be violet.

This is the strangest thing I've ever seen at a store and, naturally, I want an explanation. I start to look around again for a worker.

"Anybody here?" I shout out impatiently. "Hello?"

I receive no answer, so I help myself to my own investigation. I choose a bottle at random, an orange one, and open it to find it filled with colourful pills embossed with happy faces. I shake my head in disbelief and choose another random bottle, a red one this time, and open it nervously. This bottle is filled to the brim with a white powder. Could it be?

"Where the hell am I?" I mumble to myself, putting the bottles back with trembling hands.

This trip is no longer fun, and I begin to regret dealing myself far more Red Powder than I can handle. Maybe it's time to stop the drug cold turkey. Or maybe I'm not being fair to my old, reliable friend and am actually pregnant, and it's the baby that's driving me mad. I've read stories online about pregnant women losing their minds and some of them did mention hallucinations. What a wonderful welcome to motherhood.

Ignoring what I just saw, I hurry to the aisle with the pregnancy tests. I want to get what I came for, get out of this strange place, and take a nice, long rest under my cozy duvet.

I scan the vast selection of pregnancy tests, my hands still trembling. There is one option too many as I search nervously through the brightly coloured packages for a brand I might recognize. Just as I reach for the one to buy, I hear footsteps slowly clacking towards me.

I expect a pimpled teenager to turn the corner, greet me, and offer to explain the bizarre bottles, but the intimidating silhouette standing at the other end of the aisle clearly isn't here to help me. From the corner of my eye, I see a tall figure wearing a red shirt. I glance at him and notice a shiny gold chain around his neck. His black hair is slicked back, his eyes are hidden behind large gold-framed sunglasses, and his relaxed gait is of someone who has all the time in the world.

My cold hands are now sweating with unease. The closer he walks towards me, the louder my heart thunders, because he is not walking alone. There's something around or in him that I can't see or explain in words, but I can feel it clearly. It's the opposite of light, but it isn't quite darkness. I want to run away but now he stands so close to me I can no longer pretend I don't see him.

"Hi." I turn and acknowledge him.

He removes his sunglasses and I'm struck by some other-worldly desire that scoops out my intelligence, my morals, my shame, my footing, my entire history. He is stunning to look at. I'm suddenly as hollow as an inflatable doll; just skin tingling with lust, begging and pleading to be touched.

I have never seen a face more beautiful. I gawk at him. His eyes are mesmerizing, wide and dark, sharp at the corners and predacious like a tiger's. His thick hair is as black as coal and his smooth skin the golden brown of copper. His jaw is wide and masculine like his shoulders and his full lips are perfectly shaped. There's a scar on the right side of his neck, long and deep burgundy in colour, which only adds to his mystique.

"You look familiar," he says in his deep, soothing voice with no animation in his scruffy eyebrows.

I look into his eyes—those private, murky pools of mystery—and I wonder if I may have seen them a long, long time ago. No, that wouldn't be possible. I would never have forgotten a face like his. But why do I feel like I know him? Mixed in with my fear of him is also a strange comfort: the same comfort one would have with a childhood friend.

My throat is parched when I manage to utter, "Y-you look familiar too."

He scans me from head to toe. I don't know if he likes what he sees.

He is entirely expressionless. No smile, no gesturing with his hands, no light behind his eyes at all. The shiny gold rings on his fingers and the gold chain around his neck have more life than him.

"A lot of rain tonight," he comments and slides his hands

inside the pockets of his black dress pants, finally disarming me.

"Yeah," I smile and then I realize I'm holding the pregnancy test crassly out in front of me. I hide it behind my back and ask, "What's your name?"

"What's yours?"

"Nisha."

He walks up so close to me that I can smell his deliciously virile scent and see the outline of his strong chest against his red dress shirt. I want to take a step back but the muscles in my legs tighten. I'm dizzy, unable to move, and worried he might know my most innermost parts are throbbing at the sight of him. I didn't even know these parts in my body had the ability to throb until this moment.

He stands tall before me and I bide my time before I look up at him, the risk being him seeing right through me and into my thoughts. Disgusting, filthy, immoral, unfaithful thoughts. I want to slap myself for seeing myself in bed with this man I don't even know. I share my bed with Azar. Azar is my husband. Azar Khan is my rich, handsome, successful husband.

"I feel it too," he says.

"F-feel what?" I whimper.

A faint smile forms at the edges of his lips.

Then, as if holding up garlic to a vampire, I swiftly defend myself with a stern "I'm married."

He doesn't say anything. He continues to look at me, reading me carefully.

"I have to go." I swerve around him and force my legs to dash towards the exit.

"Bellwood," he calls out to me. "Any Friday at six."

7

FOR MONTHS LEADING up to Riad's fall wedding, I had told my mother I didn't want to go. I'd used every excuse possible, from feeling embarrassed in front of the rich kids for not having clothes as nice as they had, to finding weddings tearfully boring. I even danced around the truth and said some girls at the engagement party had been mean to me, on which my mother didn't want me to elaborate. To her I was just an ungrateful whiny teenager. My words were just air and my feelings were irrelevant.

That evening, just a few days away from Riad's wedding, my mother laid out all my salwar kameezes and sarees on the living room floor and instructed me to sit nearby. The clothes had been packed away in two familiar old suitcases fraying at the edges. They usually came out only during Eid, the only time my mother and I dressed up together.

"You can't fit into any of these, you've gotten so fat!" my mother said and shook her head and threw the clothes back into the suitcases.

Her words stung me, but they were the truth. I was no longer the slender, lithe Nisha my mother had showed off and bragged about. Puberty had a lot to do with my dimply thighs and soft stomach, but the main culprit was my new love affair with salty snacks and sugar.

After Riad's engagement party the previous winter, I was haunted by disturbing thoughts anytime I was away from the safety of my room. I began to think the whole world knew. I imagined Sonia had somehow gotten to the girls at my high school and they all believed I was a slut. I thought all the teachers thought I was a slut. I thought the boys knew and they all wanted to use me and throw me away just like Riad had done.

But the worst was that I believed all of it. I was dirty because I felt dirty. A little over a year had gone by since Riad touched me, but no matter how much time passed and how many baths I'd spent brooding in, I could never scrub the filth off.

I had strong days when I was able to lift my chin up and look people in the eye; when the angel on my shoulder told me everything was going to be fine, and I believed I could forget what had happened to me and become somebody my parents could be proud of. Those days hurt the most because they shone like a beacon of hope over an infinitely hopeless land. They pulled me up from my depths of despair and allowed me to breathe for just a moment, then dropped me to drown again.

These debilitating thoughts became so powerful that living vicariously through celebrities didn't help to stop them anymore. I searched for something else to numb myself. The Red Powder was unknown to me then and even if I knew about it, it was far too expensive for me to obtain. Kids at school sold cheap weed, of course, but I was far too timid to approach the dealers. They were all part of the popular crowd and I was the quiet wallflower.

I became addicted to the vending machines in my high school: a cheap, accessible, and quiet addiction. When the frightening thoughts crept up on me, I'd distract myself by munching away on a bag of potato chips—or two or three. When I felt sad, I'd chew gummies and guzzle pop, and revel in the sugar rush. Food was no longer something I sought when hungry. Food was an escape, an activity, a crutch.

"How many times do I have to tell you to control your eating?" my mother yelled at me as I sat on the couch with Tariq, chomping down on vanilla wafers.

Tariq was as chunky as ever; his diet consisted of three meals of white rice and whatever else my mother shoved down his throat. He didn't have to hear a belittling word about his weight because my parents couldn't care less about his looks. I was their daughter, their prize cow with the fair hide, and I had to be kept in top condition until my sale.

"You don't need to worry," I assured my mother, "I don't need anything to wear because I'm not going to the wedding anyway."

My mother ignored everything I said and nagged in Hindi, "This is all your father's fault. He never buys us anything!"

She continued sorting out clothes on the Persian carpet my father had bought. I could never forget the fight they had when my mother nagged at him to buy it.

"Any other man would've showered me with new clothes monthly!" my mother angrily threw her hands up. "And I'd have a room full of gold! Your father is cheap!"

Tariq and I didn't say anything, because we knew not to comment when our mother went on a diatribe against my father. When we were younger, we almost believed her and thought our father was the worst man ever. Now we knew she was just venting and we were fine being just a pair of ears.

But I knew something now, at the illuminating age of fourteen, that Tariq was still too young to see. My mother was the most shameless hypocrite. This was the woman who always told me not to want too many things; she said a good Muslim isn't greedy. This was the woman who lectured me for not thanking God for everything I had whenever I asked her for something new. She would declare that this life is temporary and it's Jannah that truly matters, so just be happy with whatever you have.

All this time, my mother had just tried to convince and placate herself. The reason she was angry all the time was because she wanted more in this life. She didn't want to rot in our cockroach-infested apartment, cooking, cleaning, and raising the kids of a taxi driver who simply couldn't afford to buy her anything expensive. She wanted a man like Uncle Khan, the type that would leave her with his credit cards and decorate her like a Christmas tree. My mother's greed and entitlement was why she had dragged me to the Khans' house all last year in the summer—she wanted to step into Aunty Khan's designer shoes and fantasize about being a rich man's wife.

If my mother had taken her own advice and stayed happy in her place, maybe what happened last year wouldn't have happened. If we had stayed put in the east end, gone for the usual picnics and badminton in the neighbourhood park, maybe I'd still be myself.

"There are men out there who worship their wives. They don't even let them wear the same outfit twice!" my mother went on.

"Wouldn't that be a little un-Islamic?" a sarcastic tone suddenly escaped my mouth. "I don't think God would like such wasteful displays of wealth."

My mother looked at me red-eyed and fuming, not quite sure how to respond. She was just as surprised as I was by my sudden sass.

"Shut up, Nisha," she said in English.

Tariq giggled. I obeyed my mother and shut up—habits are hard to break—but I didn't believe I had said anything wrong. Until then, I had honoured my parents blindly. Even when they did un-Islamic things, which was daily, they could do no wrong. But now the rose-coloured veil of ignorance had been yanked off from my young eyes and I saw what my parents truly were: two self-righteous sinners who had sex and forced me to live in this miserable world.

To show me who was the boss, she commanded in Hindi, "You will wear my old purple saree. You are too fat for any of the salwar kameezes, so we will just wrap the saree around you."

I looked at the purple saree she began to unfold. It had no embellishments except some design at the edge stitched with silver thread. It was heavy and opaque: the kind of fabric the older Aunties always wore on casual visits. My mother was so ashamed of my body she'd rather hide me in this hideous outfit than have me wear something that might make me feel pretty.

"I'm not wearing that," I crossed my arms and shook my head firmly, "and I'm not going to this wedding, Mom."

"Why do you kids always have to make everything so difficult?" she snapped.

"I didn't even say anything!" Tariq complained.

"What's the big deal?" I asked my mother. "I'm not feeling well so I'll just stay home while you guys go and have fun."

"People will wonder where you are."

"What people? Who on earth will care where I am?" I raised my voice.

"People talk, Nisha!" She yelled and wagged her finger at me, "You Canadian kids don't understand the meaning of reputation! Of course people will wonder why we didn't bring our daughter to the—"

"—I don't care!" I cut her off and screamed, "I don't give a fuck about your reputation!"

As soon as I shouted out the f-word, Tariq jumped away from me, showing my mother he was not on my side. I'd never used the f-word in front of my family until that evening. They both stared at me like I was an intruder, a completely unrecognizable stranger threatening them in their home.

I shrunk into the corner of the couch, afraid of what was going to happen next. My mother's eyes were red and bulging as she slowly walked towards me.

"You're swearing in my house? Right here? Right to your mother's face? Right in front of your baby brother?"

I looked into my mother's eyes firmly, ready for whatever she was going to say or do to me. I wasn't going to Riad's wedding to be mocked and laughed at by Sonia and her friends just to save my parents' precious, so-called reputation. I refused to see Riad, happy and celebrating, getting away with rape; he had murdered the best part of me. Nothing was going to change my mind—not even the fear of my raging mother.

"You're going!" she shouted as she stood over me, puffing her chest out with authority.

A bolt of frustration and anger struck me, and I grabbed a throw pillow and charged her.

"You can't make me, you bitch!" I bellowed as I thrust the pillow so powerfully my mother fell to the floor.

"You're a mean idiot!" Tariq, tearful with shock, scowled at me before running to my groaning mother.

I ran to the comfort and safety of my room, leaving them both on the floor. I turned the lights off, shut the door but didn't lock it because it was just a matter of time before my mother would come marching in there. I wished she would beat me because I deserved it for pushing her.

My pillows were wet with tears as I sobbed in disbelief over the monster I'd become. I missed the old me and I wanted desperately to resurrect that naïve child. All the kindness, curiosity, and friendliness in me had been replaced with anger, resentment, and apathy. I didn't want to live the rest of my life like this; I was just human skin around a whirlpool of darkness.

As I expected, my mother flung the door open just a few minutes later.

"Too afraid to show your face?" she sneered as she flicked the lights on.

She saw me with my face down on my pillow, crying quietly on my bed. She turned the light back off and turned on the small lamp on my nightstand. To my surprise, she sat by my hips and gently put a comforting hand on my back.

"What's wrong, Nisha?"

I had waited forever for her to ask that. I turned around and threw my arms around her waist, crying unashamedly on her lap. My mother was an angry, bitter, selfish woman but she was mine—my only mother—and I needed her protective arms.

"What's wrong, sweetie?" she asked worriedly as she began to wipe my tears.

I parted my lips to tell her everything—everything that Riad and Sonia had done—but the words were stifled by the frightening thought that they were so close to being freed. Once I'd let them out, my mother would know, and the rest couldn't be predicted. I spared myself the crippling anxiety and instead curled up like a baby next to her, clutching her thigh and digging my head into her lap.

She asked me again and again what was wrong, but I begged her to just be quiet and let me cry.

"I'm your mother, Nisha," she squeezed my hand, "you can tell me anything."

I gathered myself, wiped my tears away, and sat up. My eyes scanned the door, making sure Tariq wasn't listening through an opening.

"Riad raped me." I muttered the words fast and incoherently with my eyes fixed on my clammy palms.

My mother leaned in, not hearing what I said.

The words had been said and there was no time machine. I felt as if I'd rocketed up from the bottom of the ocean and now my lungs filled with wonderful air. My legs felt so weightless it was like they were floating over the edge of my bed. The heavy lump in my throat was no more and, out of the blue, I received the courage to look my mother in the eye.

"Riad raped me," I repeated. "He raped me."

My mother recoiled with disgust. "What are you talking about?"

"Every time you forced me to go to their house last year, he raped me in his room."

"He touched you?" she growled.

"Yes."

"Did he . . . ?"

"Yes."

My mother turned away from me and hid her face in her hands, scratching her forehead. She said nothing for a while until she suddenly interrogated me in English, "You're telling the truth, Nisha?"

"Yes."

"So, you're not a virgin anymore?"

I was shocked that my mother even knew that word and more shocked that she had blatantly used it. We never discussed sex in our family. My parents always changed the channel on TV if two people were kissing in a scene or even talking in bed. And now my mother was asking me, was I not a virgin?

There in the faint yellow light of the lamp, I saw a look of disgust, shame, and hopelessness on her face—a look that will remain with me until the day I die.

I shook my head to her question, unable to utter any word. She held back her emotions for a moment, then quietly melted down in tears. To her, a Muslim mother who genuinely believed her daughter should remain untouched until marriage, it was the end of her world. Riad had ripped the crown off my mother's head.

Watching my mother cry was a rare sight. She would cry easily while watching sappy Bollywood movies but hardly ever at real-life episodes. She was a cold woman, and I was surprised and devastated to see that coldness break down. But no matter how much it hurt to hear her sobbing, I couldn't bring myself to comfort her.

I needed her to comfort me. I needed her to hold me and tell me she would avenge me; that Riad and Sonia would not get away with what they did. I needed her to tell me I was worthy and that the thoughts of being filthy were all just in my head. I needed her to tell me she loved me no matter what.

But she did nothing.

She collected herself, wiped her tears, raised her chin, and said, "Do not tell anybody. Especially your father. Never."

"We're not going to call the police?"

"Are you crazy? Why don't we just tell the whole world you've been touched? At just twelve? Who's going to marry you then?"

I sat there, speechless. The teenage me trusted my mother would do what was best for me. She may have been bad at showing it, but she loved me, of course. There was nobody else I could run to.

"Can you promise me you won't tell anybody? Not your

brother, not your father, not your friends, not your teachers. Promise?"

I nodded. "I promise."

"You don't have to go to the wedding—I will tell your father you have a fever—but Tariq and I must go. If we don't go, your father will want to know why and so will your Aunty Khan. We will go there, eat, drop our gift, and we will never see the Khans again. I'll slowly distance myself."

I grimaced my approval but asked impatiently, "How will we make them pay? They should not get away with what they did."

"God will punish Riad one day. Let him live and you focus on your future." My mom placed a hand on my leg and smiled at me, "You are my beautiful, smart daughter. I want you to marry a rich, successful man. Don't end up like me, Nisha."

"You want me to pretend like they did nothing?"

"You must do whatever it takes to project and protect an image of being chaste and innocent. That is what a good man will want. This is for your best."

"Okay."

My mother put her arm around me, and I moved over closer to her, wanting a warmer embrace. She moved her arm away too quickly. I sat there on the bed with no words, waiting to hear what she was going to say next.

"That Riad always had a bad reputation," she snapped. "Everybody told me that, but I thought it was just gossip. I thought they were just jealous of the Khans' money. I guess money can't help you raise your kids right."

8

SIMI TRUDGES INTO my makeup studio, panting from the walk up the stairs. She drags herself along in a heavy, loose-fitting coral salwaar kameez. The dress is so baggy that it almost drowns out her ever-growing baby bump.

She examines and admires my brightly lit workspace. "So this is where the magic happens?"

No, this is where the dust gathers, but I don't tell her that.

"Do you like it? It's all Azar's design."

"I must say Azar has great taste," Simi says and lowers herself down on my chair carefully, facing me instead of the mirror. "He did marry you."

My cheeks flush and I thank her. I laugh louder than I should to hide the disgust I have for such syrupy compliments. Simi is being quite bold with her sweetness; she seems to have forgotten that subtle geniality is the only weight of our otherwise unanchored relationship.

She's suddenly come to my house tonight to get her makeup done for a party, forcing me to accept her money. She has known for years that I do makeup and not cared—just like all the other wives who just congratulated me with stiff grins—but last night she called out of the blue and practically insisted on giving me business.

"You know you don't owe me anything, right?" I tell her. "I'm happy to help you with the gala and I don't really care for the whole tit-for-tat thing."

"No, no, Nisha, please don't think that. I'm not doing you a favour; I think you do makeup amazingly and I need to look good for this party—that's the only reason I'm here."

Trying my best not to sound confrontational, I go on with collecting my brushes and pretend like I'm dumb. "I see, but you've never booked me before and I've been open for years. I don't even live that far from you so I'm just a little confused. Why now suddenly?"

Simi looks like she's been caught stealing from the cookie jar. Her round eyes enlarge with surprise and her mouth opens with the rush to find words.

"Um," she finally stutters, "do you want me to be honest?"

"Well, I don't want you to be dishonest," I laugh.

"I do love your makeup skills, but I've also just been worried about you," Simi says. "You ran out of that meeting last week with a headache—I dropped you home and you never really updated me."

"Y-you wanted to be updated?"

"Of course. Just a simple text saying you're fine or whatever would make me stop worrying. You seemed so sick that night."

I lower my chin and act busy gathering all my palettes, trying to hide my embarrassment at having judged Simi so wrongly.

"I'm sorry," I mumble, genuinely apologizing for my tendency to only see the worst in people. "I didn't want to bother you. You're pregnant and probably busy with a million things. I didn't think to message you."

"No problem." Simi accepts my apology with a warm smile and rambles on, "I know I could've been the polite one and texted you, but I didn't want to text you in case you took the pregnancy test and it came out positive—or even negative—and you were not comfortable sharing that information with me—"

"I'm not pregnant," I announce, not uncomfortable at all sharing the results of my pregnancy test with her.

What I am uncomfortable with is sharing the truths that matter. The truth that my head was hurting because my body had become dependent on the Red Powder. The truth that I need to put some of it in my tea—two or three teaspoons at least—every morning just to feel normal. The truth that I've drunk it again today not only to ward off the withdrawal pains, but also to deal with Azar continuously coming home late. The truth that when I get high, I'm unabashedly horny for that mysterious stranger at the bizarre pharmacy.

He never gave me his name, so I've named him the Red One. I don't even know if he was real or just a figment of my intoxicated imagination, but since the moment I walked away from him, the image of him in his red shirt has been floating around in my mind. I can't wash it away. I've scrubbed and I've scoured it with memories that used to soothe me: the moment Azar presented me my engagement ring, our lavish wedding, and all the other gifts he's given me. But those memories fail at overpowering the lustful thoughts in my head because, I admit, I have no emotions attached to them.

The Red One is who I saw two mornings this week when I couldn't stop touching my body. Just minutes after Azar had gone to work, I found myself excited to be alone for once. I walked into the bedroom, feeling beautiful. I disappeared under my duvet, hid away from the world, and enjoyed the touch of my own fingers without any disgust, guilt, or flashbacks of Riad.

I thank the Red One endlessly for those few moments of ecstasy and peace, but I must forget about him. He will destroy me and Azar. He will destroy all I have.

I can't tell Simi about the Red One just like I can't tell her about my addiction, and about Linda, Riad, and Sonia, but these are the big truths that are pushing against the seams of my sanity. It would be nice to unleash all these worries on a friend: a quiet friend with eager, open, nonjudgmental ears. A friend with no advice, just the willingness to be here and not cringe when I cry. I wonder if anybody in the world has a friend like that.

I look up at the brightly lit mirrors and catch a glimpse of myself: my skin is brown and all the facial features that make up Azar's beautiful wife are still intact. I return to the shallow small talk.

"Oh, so sorry to hear that, but keep trying," Simi encourages me.

"It's all right, there is no rush. It'll happen when it happens."

"Is Azar not home yet?"

It's almost eight in the evening. He didn't even bother calling me at dinner time to say he would be late. I have no idea where he is, but I've been too busy with my fantasies about the Red One that I haven't bothered to call him either.

"He's just out getting groceries, running errands," I lie.

I turn the chair so Simi faces the mirror and the lights illuminate her bare skin. She is certainly glowing—like a glazed donut high in fat.

Simi sighs before she demands, "Please go heavy with the contour. I'd like a jawline, fake or not."

"You have a jawline," I lie again, "you look great."

Simi scoffs, "Please stop; you sound like Ikram."

I begin to dab primer on her face and spread it out with my

102	SAFIA FAZLUL

fingers. The intimacy of touching her skin makes me comfortable enough to inquire about Ikram.

"What did he say?" I ask, knowing we never discuss anything negative about our husbands.

"He's just . . . " Simi pauses and thinks for a moment, "never mind."

"You can tell me."

I begin to cover the dark circles under Simi's eyes when she finally lets her guard down. It's strange to keep discussing the weather when somebody is standing so close to you that your perfumes begin blending in the air.

"He's just very happy about everything. A little too happy, you know?"

"What do you mean?"

"I mean, everything is just sunshine and rainbows, but of course it is sunshine and rainbows to him because he's not the one breaking the scale every morning."

We share a genuine, spontaneous laugh before I add, "Men are lucky they can enjoy the baby without having to carry it."

"Yes, exactly!" Simi casts a grateful look at me in the mirror. "Thank you for saying that!"

"Well, it's just a very obvious fact."

"Not to Ikram it isn't. Apparently, I'm the lucky one because I can feel the baby kick and I can have the unique memories of puking, staying up all night with heartburn, and feeling like my hips are going to split apart if I walk too fast."

I've never heard Simi complain this much. I'm enjoying her rant.

"And he keeps saying how amazing I look. I know I don't look amazing. I look bloated; I look fat. I keep telling him not to lie, but he keeps insisting he's telling the truth."

"Well, what do you want the poor guy to say?"

"I want him to admit that things—life—has changed, rapidly." Simi's voice is serious. "I want him to say he'll be here after. I want him to admit that I'm going through hell right now, but he will be here for me after our baby is born. I want him to promise he'll watch the baby whenever he can, so I can work on getting myself back."

The honesty in Simi's words is tangible and I can feel exactly what her true worry is. I'm surprised that her anxiety transfers to me because I'm usually too numb to empathize with anybody.

I take a break from brushing on her foundation and ask her with a reassuring smile, "You're worried about the future, aren't you?"

"Yeah," Simi nods before she begins to chuckle at herself. "I know it's so stupid. Billions of women have given birth and become mothers. Hundreds are out there right now pushing out a baby. It's nothing new. It doesn't make me special. I know I could ask so many friends and I could read a hundred books on it, but I'm still so unsure of what will happen once I'm a mom, you know? Am I going to be happy? Am I going to do a good job? Am I going to get my body back? Is it selfish to think that way?"

I continue doing Simi's makeup but now it feels like I'm working on somebody else's face. This person looks very attractive to me. I see the vulnerabilities and the deep thoughts behind the skin and bone, and I'm drawn to the complex beauty of it.

I owe her the same honesty she has given me, so I say with regret, "I wish I could give you advice, Simi, but I'm not in the same place as you are yet. I wish I could tell you that everything will be great, but none of us knows that for sure. But if it does end up negative, I know you'll deal with it."

"Because I'm a strong, independent woman and my husband

will help me, inshallah?" Simi says sarcastically.

I know I should say something sensitive and encouraging, but I'm enjoying this honest conversation too much. It's like a breath of fresh air hearing somebody speak their mind without any filters.

"No, because you have no choice," I tell her the truth.

We stare at each other in the mirror before we both burst out laughing.

"You are horrible at giving advice, Nisha," she says, "but thank you for listening."

9

"I HOPE MY SON gives me some good news by the end of tonight," my mother teases Azar.

My mother calls my husband her son and my husband calls my mother his mom, which means our marriage is figuratively incestuous. I never quite understood why you suddenly become your spouse's sibling after marriage. Maybe the new label is given to infantilize you; to force you to feel more liable to your spouse's family and fulfill their expectations because you are now their child. Or maybe it's given to make the image of sex less dirty in the parents' minds: instead of imagining a man thrusting into a woman, they just see a brother and sister roughhousing.

No matter what the reason is, my skin crawls at the concept. I'm always left with a bad taste in my mouth after calling Azar's mother "Mom." Her being nothing like my actual mother may also have something to do with it.

Azar's mother is a housewife too, but unlike my mother, she is an eccentric woman full of life and hobbies. She reads newspapers from back home and loves to join passionate discussions on politics; she sews, she paints, she makes specialized sweetmeats, she mixes her own masalas, and she cuts hair. She's interesting and confident—sometimes a bit too confident, just like her son.

"Yes, any good news, Nisha?" she demands.

She is a tiny woman in both weight and height, but her voice is always the grandest in the room. She never stutters or pauses midsentence because every word that leaves her mouth is well considered—even the pseudoscience, superstitions, and religion. She stands out from all the other sixty-something Aunties by wearing her salt-and-pepper hair short and dressing up in pantsuits.

We sit in Azar's parents' living room, eating appetizers and casually sipping some pre-dinner mango juice while discussing the happenings of my uterus. Azar escapes to the washroom for the third time since we got here, leaving me to sweat all alone, without any Red Powder in my system, in this pressure cooker of a conversation.

Azar's father looks uncomfortable but manages to be part of the conversation by carrying a wry smile the whole time. He is a handsome, statuesque man whom I've never seen dressed in anything but clean dress pants and impeccably ironed shirts. He is Azar's twin but with more wrinkles and a much warmer presence. He exudes a quiet confidence—the kind that matches his achievement of immigrating to Canada as a destitute student and now running his own engineering firm.

My father doesn't want to chat about pregnancy and is too tired to pretend that he does. He sits back into the armchair furthest away from the couches, hunches over his cellphone and grunts to himself. He is reading news, infuriating political news from back home to fuel the rage that is him.

My father's North American dream of a cushy job and financial freedom was never realized. He was never able to advance from being a cabdriver. When he was trying to marry me off, my mother convinced him to spend his life savings on a house to impress suitors. Now, at age sixty-six with not a single penny in his retirement fund, he's driving drunk teenagers on the weekends just to pay for a house he won't be alive to buy back from the bank.

I have offered my parents help, of course. Azar gives me a healthy monthly allowance and I always have extra to fritter away, but my father is far too proud to take money from me. My mother explained to me during a phone conversation after I left an envelope full of money under their door, that it made a man less of a man to take money from his daughter. Her lengthy lecture was so stern and discouraging that I accepted the money back, forever losing the will to help them again.

A son is fine though, and my father has no problem putting his hand out to Tariq. My little brother was shipped off to Alberta for manual labour years ago and expected to send money regularly. My mother justifies taking a third of her son's hard-earned money by claiming it will prevent him from buying haram things.

Tariq grew up from a chubby boy with bad grades to a fat young man with very few career prospects. His only passion in life was smoking weed and that fateful day when my mother found his naked-lady-shaped bong, he was told to find a job in a different province, spread his wings, become a man, and so on. Ironically, when I was told to leave the nest, the only possibility discussed was marriage. To my parents, a son's freedom was not equal to a daughter's freedom: sons flew away as high and as far as they could, while daughters were to be tied to somebody's else's son.

"These spring rolls are amazing, Mom," I lie to Azar's mother to avoid answering her question.

I could just answer truthfully, "No, sorry, I'm not pregnant," but I'm deeply conflicted with the idea of apologizing for something I can't control. Also, the last thing I need is to hear my mothers' upset grunts echoing my own disappointment. I, too, wish I was pregnant now. Now more than ever—with or without the pains of my past being acknowledged—I wish I was pregnant with my husband's baby so I could continue to roll mindlessly around the wheel of life. There is no other way to forget about the Red One and have my perfect life back on track.

"Nothing yet," I give up and declare reluctantly, blushing as I indirectly announce to my father that I had sex.

As expected, the two mothers flip up their hands in disappointment like their favourite cricket team just lost the match. They might as well just boo and throw their drinks at me.

Azar finally returns from the washroom and plops down on the couch, rubbing his hands together in anticipation of his mother's spring rolls. If it were I who made him an appetizer dripping with oil, I'd never hear the end of it.

"Something wrong with your bladder?" I whisper to him as our mothers rave about how the purpose of life is having babies.

"No, why?" Azar looks clueless.

I mutter through a grin, "You keep hiding in the washroom leaving me here alone. You know I don't want to be alone with them."

"I had to pee." Azar grins to detract attention from our bickering.

"Three times in one hour?"

"Can't a man even pee without his wife nagging?"

"I'm not nagging, I'm—"

"What are my sweethearts talking about?" my mother calls

out from the couch across us.

"Oh, nothing," Azar smiles flirtatiously, "we were just talking about how beautiful you look tonight, Mom."

My mother blushes, as Azar's parents throw their heads back and laugh at their terribly charming son. My father looks up from his cellphone and attempts a laugh too. His laughter, a rare occurrence, sounds more like a stifled cough.

"Don't be shy, my dears," Azar's mother singsongs to us like we are little children, "anything you can say to each other, you can say to us."

My mother nods in agreement and dares to add, "We are a family. There should never be any secrets in a family."

She quickly shifts her eyes away from mine. She knows exactly what I'm thinking. She knows she should be ashamed to ever lecture me about secrets. It is her fault Riad and Sonia are somewhere out there, going on about their day, living worry-free in some big house with a pool in the backyard, being rewarded instead of punished for the crime they committed—the crime that's never stopped punishing me.

My mother is just a lonely woman now; her only companions are the roses in her garden. She still dyes her hair black, chasing the youth that left her as fast as all the Aunties that were her supposed friends. Seventeen years ago, after I told her about what Riad had done, she quit being a social butterfly. She isolated herself in our apartment, reading the Quran all day in between cooking meals and cleaning. She chose to immerse herself in a world where nothing mattered but the ancient texts as if she were finished with this world and ready for the afterlife.

After living most of my life with a cold and invulnerable mother, I'm having difficulty adjusting to this new warm and inviting lady she has slowly transformed into. Whereas she only spoke to me to tell me dinner was ready, she now calls me almost every other day and begs for Azar and me to visit. With Tariq gone and my father working all day, she has nothing left except TV and the threatening tick-tock of the clock.

"We were just talking about how excited we are for dinner." Azar smacks his hands together, "Is it ready yet, Mom? We actually have to get going sooner than I expected."

For once, my husband appears more eager than me to leave his parents' place. I watch him fidget with the crease in the thigh of his pants as his foot taps with impatience. He must have some important work project to finish.

Azar's mother rises and motions for everybody to march into the kitchen where her special chicken dish has finally finished baking. We usually dine at their kitchen table because there is no separate room to host dinner.

Azar's parents live in a smallish house in an exceptionally good neighbourhood just a fifteen-minute drive away from us. Although they could easily afford a massive home had they moved out a little further west, they decided—like many other immigrants with rags-to-riches stories—to choose security over pomp. They are a humble couple who rarely display their wealth, which is probably why they allowed one of their three well-to-do sons to marry a cab driver's daughter.

I ask Azar's mother if she needs any help preparing the table and of course I'm met with an indignant headshake. My mother stays back at the kitchen counter to cut lemons and I leave to sit next to Azar at the kitchen table. He is in deep conversation with our fathers about the perfect way to barbeque a steak. The three of them disagree and soon a relaxed discussion turns into an aggressive debate.

"Quiet now! We can discuss this next time we have a barbeque," Azar's mother roars at the men as she swiftly puts down a large bowl of salad before going back to the counter.

Azar and his father back down gracefully but my father continues to berate people who cut the steak while it's on the grill, daring to destroy its moisture.

"Dad, it's really not a big deal," I try to reason with him. He ignores me and states that some people are just not fit to ever come near a barbeque grill.

Azar's father begins to look offended when finally my mother brings a piping hot plate of chicken biryani and tells my father sternly in Hindi, "We are here to eat a meal as a family—not to fight over nonsense."

"You go mind your business in the kitchen," my father dismisses her with a wave of his hand, "let us men discuss in peace."

My mother complies and I immediately feel a sense of déjà vu. Every single dinner party I'd ever been to, whether it was at Azar's parents', my parents', or at any other Aunty and Uncle's house, the women always hustled in the kitchen while the men sat around and chatted up a storm, awaiting their hot meals. The men never offered to help serve and, oddly enough, the women looked on with pride when their husbands and sons gulped down their food.

I haven't yet become the overworked wife with oil burns on her hands and sweat running down her forehead but that is my future and it's unavoidable. There will be a day, when we finally have children, when Azar will talk about the importance of tradition and nutrition and force me to cook every single meal from scratch. There will be a day when we will fight and he will refuse to pay for catering—just because he has the power to do so—and force me to cook for a bevy of guests. They say everybody eventually turns into their parents and we're no exception.

I gaze at Azar, my modern, Canadian-raised, educated

husband, sitting there and entertaining my crazy father while his mother struggles to find a coaster for the heavy pot of nihari in her hands. I place one right before her as quickly as I can, and she hurries away to get more dishes. I float away amidst the chaos and wonder if Azar will take care of me when I'm old. My mother always said that daughters-in-law take care of old parents and so I wonder what I'll do if my future son marries somebody smart enough not to choose that fate.

My mind begins to race again and thoughts whirl around like a leaf caught in a storm. My mother and mother-in-law continue to bring the food and drinks while the men move on to politics. The whole scene begins to upset me.

"I'm going to the washroom," I excuse myself.

Azar doesn't hear me because he is too busy talking. He doesn't even notice me getting up to leave.

Instead of going to the washroom closer to the kitchen, I decide to go to the one upstairs to give myself more time away from my handlers. The stairs are in the living room where the coffee table is still full of appetizers and empty glasses. I go to grab a pakora, warm and rich like the comfort I need, when I hear something vibrating from under the couch Azar and I were sitting on.

Azar must've dropped his cellphone and so I bend down to fetch it. A private number is calling and I decline it because it's a Sunday evening and it couldn't be anybody but a telemarketer. The incoming call screen disappears and I see there are six new message notifications from Linda. Do I want to know? Do I already know?

I put the phone down and rapidly discuss with myself in my head. I tell myself I should respect my husband's privacy and not read his messages. She's probably just messaging because they have work tomorrow and she needs help with something.

333

I tell myself I'm just an emotional, pathetic, paranoid wreck and Azar deserves better; he deserves to be trusted. I blame myself in any way I can—present any argument that will stop me from opening those text messages—but I fail to protect myself. I don't want to hurt myself, but I must check the messages.

The first picture is of her lying down on her bed, loose blonde hair posed over a pink satin pillow, one breast hidden in her black lace bra and the other bare and cradled in her manicured hand.

I really miss you tonight.

Are you sure you can't come over? Not even for an hour?

The fourth message is a picture of what's in between her legs. Ready and available without the bankrupting wedding, the ovulation strips, the daily nagging, the fake happy pictures splashed all over social media.

She misses you too, baby. Don't you wanna give her some attention?

Ok, I guess you're busy with your wife. I'll see you tomorrow at work, xoxo.

I quiver uncontrollably. Every corner of me is hot with blood, burning with restraint, and I must sit down before I erupt. I want to turn this coffee table over so every single glass and plate shatters into pieces on the floor. I want to break the TV with anything I can get my hands on. I wanna kick the couches until my toes bleed. I want to show our mothers and fathers these obscene pictures before hurling the phone right at Azar's ugly face. But I won't. I can't.

Truth is not truth if it remains in the dark. I won't be the one to shine the light on the end of my marriage. I have nothing else in this life except my marriage. My marriage is not just the shiny diamond on my ring finger; my marriage is my income, my social life, my identity. I'm Nisha, the beautiful wife of Azar. He's Azar, the handsome, successful, faithful husband of Nisha. We were supposed to be perfect.

There must be an explanation. She's harassing my husband. I look at her messages again to see what she wrote before but everything prior has been deleted. What did Azar say to her? Did he say he loves her? Did he tell her we're trying to have a baby? I begin to cry.

I hear footsteps approaching. I mark all the messages as unread and throw the cellphone under the couch where I found it. I wipe away the tears, but they just won't stop rolling down my burning cheeks. I force myself to be twelve years old again, back in Riad's room, and allow the shock to freeze me. The tears stop now.

"There you are," Azar waltzes into the room, "you just disappeared."

I can't bring myself to say anything to him. I stuff a pakora into my mouth, and then another.

"I can't find my phone, babe. I think you're sitting on it," he says casually.

His arrogance won't allow him to think of the possibility of me getting to his phone before him. Or perhaps he suspects it but is giving a great performance of cluelessness. He's clearly an actor of the highest calibre.

He dares placing his hand on my shoulder. His touch disgusts me and I spring up reflexively.

"I was hungry," I mumble through a mouthful of pakoras only to stick another one in. "I'll be in the kitchen."

"You just ate!" Azar exclaims as he gets on the ground to see under the couch.

I watch him on his knees. I imagine her under him, pulling him in, kissing him. My stomach turns and I must look away before I vomit.

"Found it!" he laughs and follows me.

He catches up with me, grabs my hand suddenly, and squeezes it. I don't move my hand because that would be suspicious but I'm completely unable to squeeze his hand back. The last sliver of dignity left in me won't allow me to grip his hand. "You're acting strange tonight." Azar kisses my knuckles. "Is something wrong?"

"Nothing." I smile. "Nothing is wrong."

We enter the kitchen where our mothers have finally finished bringing out all the dishes. They sit together and lean their heads at us like one would do to a cute puppy or baby.

"Come eat, you adorable couple!" Azar's mother orders us.

My mother points to two plates overflowing with food and smiles, "I have already served you, my kids."

10

THE OLD NEIGHBOURHOOD looks as if I never left it. They stuck a few condo buildings here and there to make it look pretty, but it's still the same cold, barren battleground where every day is a fight to keep your dreams alive and your dignity intact. I haven't been to this part of town in over a decade. I was hoping I'd never have to.

I didn't want to take Victoria out here and make myself a target for attention or a carjacking, so I'm sitting in the back of a taxi now with a driver who reminds me of my father when he was younger. He has a strong accent and doesn't speak much because he is focused on driving as quickly as possible.

The working class is out working and the streets are empty except the odd drunk hobbling to nowhere. We drive by stores and diners that awake memories. These were the streets I'd walk on for hours when I couldn't bear the pain of what Riad did to me. These were the joints I'd go to buy greasy fries drenched in ketchup—all I could afford back then with the quarters in my pocket—when my parents were having a loud, scary fight. This was once the setting of a lonely life with no hope for something better.

Just like the neighbourhood, I look a little more polished but not much has changed. I'm just as lonely as ever and nothing ever gets better.

I don't even know exactly what I'm doing here. This morning, I chugged down my laced tea and tried to ignore all the pictures of Azar and me all over the house, but the happy couple in the frames kept observing my every move, haunting and heckling me as I cried. I decided I had to leave the house and go anywhere else.

I put the darkest kohl around my eyes, the most seductive China pink on my lips, and an attention-grabbing amount of blush on my cheeks. I slid into an immodest pair of tight jeans, a silky black low-cut camisole, and a pair of tan platform heels fit for a streetwalker. I straightened my hair and let it loose over my exposed shoulders, free to run wild with the wind. Today, I did not want to look like Nisha, the good Indian, Muslim housewife. Today, I wanted to look available and desirable for the ghost I came here to chase: the Red One. I have nobody else to go to.

I had convinced myself he was indeed just a figment of my imagination. The Red Powder had me high as a kite that night and I probably just saw what I wanted to see: a striking man who would extend his hand and rescue me from this boring, cruel life sedated with phony happiness. But then I discovered that the hotel he said he'd be at, the Bellwood Inn, does indeed exist.

According to the Internet, the Bellwood Inn is right here in this neighbourhood in a little corner in the east end. There's a small hope I'll see the dark-haired stranger with the piercing eyes again. I have all the time in the world to search. Anything is better than staying home all day, smelling Azar's cologne in the air. I've avoided him all week; told him I have a terrible cold and slept alone in the guest bedroom so he wouldn't touch me. I can't look at him anymore. I can't cook for him or do his laundry without hating myself.

The driver turns into a street not too far from the apartment building of my childhood. There was a girl in high school I had a science project with and she lived here in one of these old bungalows. We visited each other often to finish our presentation. She was kind, funny, and loved biology as much as I did. She invited me over once when the project was done but of course I distanced myself and never spoke to her again.

My feeling of loneliness deepens as we drive past her house. I suddenly remember there was a small strip mall at the end of the street and a motel hidden somewhere near there. I must've seen the tacky vacancy sign of that motel a thousand times because my bus to high school drove right by it. Yes, it suddenly comes back to me, there was an old, faded sign at the entrance of a parking lot that read The Bellwood Inn.

I remember the bus ride clearly now. I always had pop songs playing loudly in my earphones to block the world out. And now come the long-buried pictures of high school: flashes of happy, normal teenagers playing sports and laughing with their friends while I hide away in the library or in some washroom stall. I wonder why the Red One picked this tiny, unknown dump out of all the hotels and motels in the city. I wonder why he guided me to the place that would cue one terrible memory after another.

The driver stops the car and unlocks my door impatiently at the parking lot of the motel. The building is an L-shape of connected rooms, all on the ground level. He zooms away and I'm left alone. There's a single car in the small parking area, a rusty old sedan with its back door held together with duct tape. There is no way a man with as much poise as the Red

One would drive around in this thing. It doesn't belong to him because he isn't here because he doesn't exist.

"This is crazy." I talk to myself. "I've lost my mind."

I want to turn around and take the bus to the nearest station, hop on a cab, go home and just accept life like millions of women do. Husbands cheat. Just live with it. Don't break up a family, don't hurt my aging parents, don't ruin our reputations, and definitely don't bite the hand that feeds me. It won't be that bad. I'll just take the Red Powder every day; have an extra strong cup before sex and sweet dinner dates and romantic vacations and go to my grave high and happy. I've faked everything up until now anyway.

Just as I'm ready to swallow the last crumbs of my pride and dignity, I'm pulled to the door of the check-in which is only distinguishable from the other rooms because of a vacancy sign. I don't know what's driving me—maybe it's curiosity, maybe it's the reluctance to go back home, or maybe it's sheer desperation just to see that beautiful face again.

I open the door and enter a shoebox of a room so dark I must squint to see what's inside. A strong whiff of mildew mixed with a scent of stale cigarettes overpowers my senses and I begin to cough. To the left of me, behind the glass screen of a small reception table, a boney white man in his forties looks up at me closely. He has a dark ponytail and scrawny tattoo-covered arms emerging from his black tank top. He disappears into the room behind him without a word.

To the right, on an old couch with the gaudiest floral print, a dark figure sits with his right ankle crossed over his left knee. My heart races as I recognize those intense eyes.

"I knew you'd come." The Red One looks at me with effortless seduction.

He is wearing a red shirt and black pants just like the last time, but he's freshly shaved and his hair is combed back into a ponytail. He looks even more striking than I remembered, like a dark painting at a museum that stops you in your tracks, grasps your full attention, and imbues you with such strong emotion that you just can't look away.

I am too afraid to walk closer to him. My desire for him is so powerful and so alien that it frightens me. I'm hoping he will say something funny or anecdotal to relax me, but he just stares at me for a moment with complete silence. He's as impermeable as a brick wall, but I think I see something that resembles pity in his eyes.

"You can leave if you want," he says monotonously, not revealing whether he wants me to stay or go. "You're free to choose."

I know I can still leave. I can leave and forever pretend today didn't happen. I can return to my life and my husband and let time allow me to forget this fantasy. I can, as I've done my whole life, kill and bury what I want to because it satisfies the moral ideologies of others.

Or I can stay. I can stay and satisfy what I genuinely need. I can stay and lose to lust: an opponent I've never had the pleasure to fight.

Until this pivotal moment I've been living separately from my own sex drive. I was introduced to sex through rape and acquainted with it through wifely duty. My mother always said to save myself for my husband, but she never explained how to save myself from my own urges. My sex drive was stolen from me, it was never acknowledged and never understood, but the body that was harbouring it—the skin, the bones, the breasts, the hips—was always treated as strictly sexual. Cover it up, hide it like the dirty taboo object it is, and only give it away as a present to the man who'll legally sign up to use it as an incubator.

The lust I feel for this stranger before me makes me feel like my soul is attached to my body for once. I feel alive for the first time since those selfish childhood days. Children act on emotion, not cunning schemes and ulterior motives. There's nothing I want from this man except him. I absolutely don't want to marry him, I don't want his money, I don't want to show him off on the Internet, I don't even want to use him to get even with my husband . . . I just want him inside me and there's no worldly explanation why.

"I'll stay."

A slight nod tells me he approves of my decision. I notice the watch on his wrist because it glimmers with every move of his hand. It is worth thousands. His shoes are designer, and his clothes are too streamlined to be cheap. Now I'm utterly confused about his car and his choice of hotel.

"That's your car out there?" I ask, my nose scrunched up.

"No." He gets up and reaches out his right hand. "Would you turn around and leave if it was?"

I give him my hand and my heart leaps as soon as he touches me. With my cheeks red with shame, I shake my head to his question. Not a chance, I think to myself. He could be driving a cardboard box with plastic wheels attached to it and I'd still walk from the other corner of town to this seedy motel just to hold his hand. And I thought I knew myself.

"This place is . . . " I look around the dark room and see the stained wallpaper peeling at the seams, " . . . scary."

He lets go of my hand and brazenly puts his arms around my waist, pulling me closer to him.

"But do you feel safe?"

His arms and his grip are strong—amazingly strong—almost supernaturally. I nod as nervousness and excitement form an involuntary smile on my face. I've never felt such desire to touch anybody. I want to touch his face, the scar on his neck, explore every curve and recess, trace his lips before I lose myself in kissing them, but instead I take a step back.

"I don't even know your name," I laugh. "This is crazy."

The Red One removes his hands from my waist. I expect he will tell me his name now, where he's from, what he does for a living, and maybe his age and, if he's as shameless as I am, his marital status. But he doesn't reveal a single thing.

"What do you want me to do?" he asks.

"Do what you want to me." The words escape and I bite my lower lip as if instinctively trying to stop myself from talking. "Do anything you want."

"Are you sure?"

"Yes."

A slight smirk forms on his lips and I'm immediately nervous about what I just said to him. He takes out a key from the back pocket of his black jeans and hands it to me.

"Room six." He motions for me to leave and says abruptly, "I have to do some business with my friend here. I'll be there in five minutes."

I do as he says without any questions. His tone is arrogant but straightforward. He's not the romantic type, I gather, but that's acceptable because it's not romance I want from him.

My eyes are blinded by the bright daylight as I step outside again. I quickly put on my oversized sunglasses to hide my face. I can see our room is right across the reception and so I walk to it quickly, peeking in every direction because I'm terrified that somebody is watching me.

I put the key in the keyhole and turn the rattling knob, pursing my lips with dislike. I have never been to a room this ancient and dingy. Azar and I don't stay at any hotel ranked less than five stars. I have never opened the door to a tiny bed with a greasy headboard next to a broken closet, a TV that looks retro, and a nightstand with a leg missing—all on a squeaky floor and under a depressing stench reminiscent of joblessness and hopelessness.

But I do know that stench. I had run away so far that I had almost forgotten these were once my surroundings. I don't miss the old apartment building and the old hood and I'd rather die than go back, but I'm also strangely nostalgic for the simplicity of those days. When I was young and poor, happiness was as uncomplicated as a candy bar from the dollar store and my life goal was easy to define because it was the same as everybody else's in the ghetto: survive, get out of here, and make money.

But once you're out and the almighty dollar has supposedly elevated you, identifying your ambitions and your struggles become your own unique enemy. Once the problems are no longer financial, they are in your mind. You waste hours worrying about the tiny wrinkles on your forehead, what to wear to yet another party—impressing people you despise—all while feeling guilty for not knowing if your problems are really problems at all.

I take a deep breath and realize that this is not a dirty motel room. This is the next best thing to lying on the wet grass and watching the rainbow that greets everybody for free. I'm closer to the ground than I have been in a long time. I remove my platform sandals and sit at the edge of the bed. There's a quilt underneath me with cigarette burns and what appears to be a long, red strand of hair. I flick the hair away and lie down on the bed, oblivious of the bed bugs that are probably snug in the mattress.

The curtains are drawn, but the strong sunlight illuminates the room brighter than I'm comfortable with. I want to be with the Red One in the dark because the dark hides my imperfections, veils the emotions in my eyes, and alleviates my guilt. I do feel extreme guilt. Even though this is exactly what Azar deserves, I hate myself for doing this to him. But I can't stop.

I slide under the quilt and hide my face in the lumpy pillow, my body tingling, throbbing, and wet with anticipation.

I hear the doorknob turn and peek up from underneath the quilt. He steps inside with his commanding gait, shuts the door behind him, and places his cellphone on the TV stand. We are all alone here now in the dark. Only the singing birds outside know I am here inside these four walls, hiding away from my life, free to be naked.

He stands at my feet and asks me, "Do you like the Red Powder?"

"Yeah," I nod. "I like it a lot."

He reaches into his front pocket and takes out a small red box.

My heart beats faster and I wonder what he's doing. I sink deeper into the bed and pull the quilt up to my chin.

"Swallow," he says.

I look up at him nervously, but then he hands me a red pill that resembles a mint.

"What is this?"

"The Red Powder in its purest form."

If you aren't supposed to take candy from a stranger, you most certainly aren't supposed to take drugs. I know this and I'm not naïve, but I also trust this stranger. I feel like I know him. There is no logic at all behind this strong trust but it's just as tangible as my lust for him.

"I need water." I hesitate as I take the pill from him, shivering slightly as our fingers touch.

He reaches into his back pocket and hands me a silver hip flask.

"I don't really drink."

"It's water," he says, then opens the flask and gulps down a pill to put me at ease.

"Oh," I smile. "I'll have it then."

I swallow the pill and hand back the flask in anticipation. I've never had the concentrated Red Powder pills. They're expensive because they're rare, and they're rare because they're illegal. While the legal diluted powder makes you optimistic about life, the pills make you excited—so excited that you could die from a heart attack.

I don't fear what my reaction will be. I'll either live, which will be the most likely outcome because I've developed a high tolerance for the stuff, or I'll die. Death is inevitable for everyone, and while I'm fearful of what's on the other side, I'm also ready to face it. My marriage is over. Even though it keeps going, it is over. I have little to live for now, but a painful future of fake greetings and forced sex.

The Red One glances at his watch and wastes no time to unbutton his shirt. His honey-coloured body is hard and muscular. He could probably lift me up with one arm, no sweat.

"Take your clothes off," he says softly, but firmly.

I fidget with the bottom of my camisole before gently pulling it up and then finally taking it off. The throbbing between my legs intensifies as I watch him staring at me in my red lace bra. I want to unhook it for him, but my arms freeze. I see flashes of Azar's face—the only face that has seen me naked since my rapist—and the guilt becomes a rock in my stomach.

"I don't know if I should do this," I whisper into my chest so he can't see the tears well up in my eyes.

"Do what you want." He stands still at the foot of the bed and says, "You're free to choose."

The pill begins its spell on me as I sit with my hands covering my cleavage. I begin to feel giddy and unafraid. I look at the shirtless sculpture of a body before me and I know what I want to do. I stare, unashamedly, at his gorgeous face and I know what choice I want to make. I must have him.

I nod his way and he removes his shoes and undoes his leather belt. His black dress pants fall to the floor, and he finally walks towards me with a magnificent bulge in his black briefs. He peels the quilt off me and throws it over the bed. I pull up to my knees and dare to caress his strong thighs and the naked skin right above his underwear.

He slips his hands under my bra straps and slides them over my shoulders, allowing my breasts to hang above the lace cups. He cups them gently with his large, knowing hands, tweaking my nipples with increasing intensity. I clench the muscles in my thighs to stop myself from exploding as I succumb to him entirely.

I get off the bed and hurriedly take all my clothes off as he takes his briefs off. He's almost supernaturally large and perfect, like the rest of him. I wrap my arms around him; grab onto him like he's the rock saving me from falling off a cliff. My head only reaches his chin as I sink deep into his chest and rest in the cozy warmth of his skin on my skin. I feel a powerful sense of belonging. I feel like the rest of my life was just time wasted wandering around to finally reach this moment.

He only hugs me back briefly before lifting my chin up with his finger so our eyes meet. He bends down slightly, I stand on my tiptoes, and we kiss. We kiss passionately and I can't help but moan as his hands explore every curve on my body. I kiss his chin, his chest, the burgundy scar on his neck. His hands stop at my hips and pull me closer to him aggressively. I feel his hardness and I can't contain myself any longer.

"Take me." I beg him. "I need you."

I return to the bed, lying down on my back, astounded by

the sight of his dark figure appearing above me. The sunlight creates a glow around him and the vision is as dizzying and grand as a night sky full of stars. I'm high and starving for him, but I can't confine the ominous feelings that creep up on me. No matter how pleasurable life is in the present, the pain of the past always grips me by the ankles.

The Red One wraps his strong arms around me and envelops me with his weight. My body feels like it's in a vice and I'm completely immobile. His muscular legs pin mine down as I feel powerless and taken, just like I did with Riad. Riad always wins. No matter how badly I want to be here to experience this passion, this forbidden delight, my mind wants to leave.

I shut my eyes and disappear into the darkness. He enters me slowly. His length seems endless as he fills every bump and fold of me. I'm full of him as I float away in ecstasy—a trance of bliss I can only revel in for seconds before I force myself to stop. I begin to think about how I will get home after this, the weather, a movie I watched years ago. I leave my body behind because it disgusts me. My body disgusts me.

With my eyes shut tight, I feel him lowering himself and shrouding me. He's so close to me that I'm wearing his skin and his breath touches my face. His fingers dance on my neck before he grabs it suddenly.

I've never been in a chokehold, and I'm surprised at how much it's exciting me. He's removing my responsibility from this disgusting act. He's reducing me to a desirable thing, detaching the emotions and thoughts that taunt me daily; stripping off me the roles and the responsibilities I never truly wanted; destroying the ridiculous always-politically-correct, chit-chatting, floral-skirt-wearing, omelette-making suburban trophy wife phony I've allowed myself to become. He's handing me my rebellion.

"Look at me," he demands.

I hear him but I can't do it.

"Look at me!" he commands as his grip tightens.

I open my eyes briefly and look everywhere but at him. If I look into his eyes, I'll stop floating in the weightless clouds that protect me and fall right into the earth.

He releases my neck and begins to kiss and lick my neck lovingly before he whispers into my ear, in the most caring tone, "You need to face it."

Now I open my eyes wide.

"Face what?" I pull back from his kisses and ask him sternly.

He answers me with his tongue in my mouth, kissing me deeply as he shoves into me. He pauses to lock eyes with me, and I finally submit to every sensation. For the first time in my life, I allow myself to feel. I surrender to the pleasure that vibrates throughout me with his every thrust, I inhale the manly scent of his skin. I melt into his warmth. I become myself by becoming his.

Through my moaning, I somehow spurt out, "I'm yours."

I tell him those two words because, for the first time in my life, I belong. There's no mimicking of emotions here. There's no behaving robotically to just please somebody. I want to be here, wholeheartedly. I wish I could be here forever.

"You've always been mine," he whispers as he pulls himself out of me. "Turn around."

I don't understand what he means but I'm too eager for him to re-enter me to care. I turn around and face the pillow with my hands clutching the sheets beneath, giving him full control. He lunges into me forcefully and I jump at the pain which might just as well be pleasure. The lines are blurred but I need to feel him desperately. I beg and moan for more of him, no matter how intense his touch.

He yanks my hair and nips the back of my neck while pounding himself into me. I'm shocked by the violent things I've never had done to me and wholly surprised at how much it's exciting me. It's like he knows exactly what I like and what I need to be present. Even before I knew it myself.

My eyes water with tears of both fulfillment and fear. I cry because these stolen moments are not mine to keep or control or schedule. I cry because all the money, pretty clothes and jewellery in my life have lost their sheen now that I've met this rare human being. I cry because this might be the greatest pleasure in the world. And now that I've experienced it, how will I ever live without it?

He flips me around again and I stare at him with admiration. I could worship him. He thrusts into me again but this time he uses his finger to help stimulate me. His every rub, every brush, every stroke elevates me further and further to a place of bliss I've never been with somebody watching.

He continues, at a pace he somehow knows is perfect to me. My body is in such pleasure I think I'm floating above the bed. He continues to touch me and I continue to rise, I call out to God, dig my nails into his back, and enter heaven.

Seconds after, I feel him releasing himself inside me, filling me with his warmth. He removes himself from me and drops down next to me. We lie shoulder-to-shoulder, staring at the ceiling while catching our breaths. I bask in harbouring a part of him while I'm still flying, but as soon as I come down, reality slaps me in the face.

"I'm not on any birth control," I warn him.

"Nothing will happen," he says matter-of-factly, and his tone doesn't invite any questions.

His dark eyes glimmer like black opals in the sunlight as he turns to look at me. "You can trust me."

I scoff, "We don't even know each other. You're a stranger."

"You can't trust a stranger?"

"Well, no." I pretend like I don't trust him because he doesn't need to know the absurdity that I do and explain, "That's kind of the reason behind regarding somebody as a stranger: you don't know their intentions."

"You're right." The Red One nods and looks away from me for a moment before staring right at me again and sighing, "You can't trust strangers but it's usually the ones closest to you that hurt you the most."

I nod in agreement and think nothing of his words. He keeps his eyes glued on me and I realize he is talking about Azar cheating. Chills run right through me as I nearly jump away from him with goosebumps all over my naked body. It's not possible that he knows what Azar did.

"Who are you?" I demand.

The Red One stretches his arms out indifferently and springs up after yawning. "I have to get going."

"What's your real name? Have we met before?" I nag, pressing for his attention, but he gathers his clothes swiftly and disappears into the washroom.

I'm left alone in the bed dreading the reality of him leaving me soon. I don't want him to go.

He comes out of the washroom fully dressed and scrambles to find his shoes.

"You didn't answer my questions," I say.

He puts his shoes on and finally looks at me dismissively, "You're high and paranoid. Stay here for another thirty minutes and you'll be good to go."

"Do you have to leave so soon?"

He picks the quilt up from the floor and covers me with it. "I have to go."

"Will I see you again?"

"Do you want to?" He smirks.

I swallow my pride. "I really want to see you again. Please?"

"You will soon."

"We don't have each other's numbers."

"I'll find you," he promises with his eyes.

"How?" I truly wonder.

Before he gets to answer me, his cellphone rings loudly. He bends down and kisses me with his tongue, making my heartbeat fast again, before he grabs his cellphone and heads for the door.

"I'll find you," he repeats before disappearing to the world outside.

11

I MAKE AZAR'S ORGANIC brown free-range eggs. Two whites, one yolk, fried in olive oil and not runny. But, for the first time ever in five years, I add some thyme and cayenne pepper. Three days have passed since I saw the Red One. He has disappeared and he's taken me with him. The last three mornings, I've been waking up with somebody else's feelings. I recognize the face in the mirror, but my skin feels constantly cold and something has shifted within me. Either I'm lacking something or I have gained something. I don't know which it is, but I know I'm not the same. I may still look like her, but I'm no longer Nisha.

I place Azar's plate and utensils on the table, next to his cold glass of grapefruit juice, and I sit down with a glass of water and a handful of peanuts that serve as my breakfast.

I've had no appetite since I've tasted the Red One's lips. In between staring at my phone waiting for him to text me and daydreaming about touching him again, I've been nibbling on nuts, cheese, and chocolate the past three days. A good meal doesn't appeal to me anymore. Neither do showers, nor dressing up, nor socializing with all the phonies in my life. All I want and need is him.

"Good morning, gorgeous." Azar comes whistling into the kitchen.

He's in the happiest of moods. He must be seeing Linda tonight.

I force a smile his way before returning to my cellphone.

"Nisha?"

"Yeah?"

"Why are you dressed like that?" Azar asks in the background.

His voice has become like the buzzing of a fly to me; I hear it loud and clear but pay it no attention.

"Dressed like what?" I mumble as I stare at my phone, searching the Internet for pharmacies with a red neon sign nearby.

I'm hoping to find the elusive pharmacy where I first met the Red One. If I find it, I'll stand right in front of it every single day until he comes driving by.

"You look like a bag lady," he raises his voice to get my attention, "all you need is a cart full of garbage."

I look down to see what I'm wearing. I had mindlessly thrown on whatever was easiest to grab in my closet this morning. The result was one of Azar's oversized t-shirts and some cheap leggings I usually wear as underpants in the winter. I don't look as sultry and elegant as I usually do in one of my silk robes, but I don't look as bad as Azar's repulsed looks are suggesting.

"It's eight in the morning and I'm home. Who's going to see me?"

"I am," Azar says as he takes a bite from his plate.

I resist the urge to throw my glass at him and smile coyly, "I'm just not in the mood to dress up today, honey."

"You're having one of those days again?" Azar rolls his eyes. "Did you call that damn head doctor? I gave you his number a long time ago."

"No, I will . . . if I need to. I'm fine right now," I say confidently. "I think I'll be just fine from now on—"

"These eggs taste different . . . " Azar chews his food like a cow in pasture, " . . . I like them."

"I added something extra. Thought you'd like something new."

"It's delicious, but I like the usual eggs." Azar grins widely the way I used to think adorable but now just makes him look like a goofy camel. "You know me, I'm always happy with what I have."

I can't bear to respond to this vile, disgusting liar I call my husband. I wonder if he's saying such words to taunt me or if his guilt is driving him to utter them. It's probably the former because Azar is incapable of feeling any guilt.

"You don't look sick anymore," Azar mumbles while chewing, "I think it's time we started trying again. Babies don't make themselves."

"Yeah. Sure."

"You're not very talkative this morning."

"Yeah." I look up at him, annoyed that my Internet search failed, and then ask, "You haven't been to a pharmacy around here with a bright red sign? Maybe ten or so minutes away—in the middle of nowhere?"

"What?"

"It's smallish and in a place with no other stores around; no houses or apartment buildings. Hardly any traffic on the streets around it. It's not far from the highway. You can see the sign as you exit—"

"No, I don't know what place you're talking about," Azar shakes his head and rises from the table, leaving his empty plate and glass for me to clean up as usual. "But I'm happy you're taking Victoria out and seeing places. Just don't scratch her."

"I wouldn't dare."

I sit and wonder about this phantom pharmacy that isn't listed anywhere and doesn't show up on any aerial map of the neighbourhood. It's almost as if it vanished along with the Red One.

"What are you thinking so hard about?"

I snap out of my thoughts, but don't respond to him. My eyes fix on his glass and plate. Putting food and drink on them is a fifteen-minute job and taking them to the dishwasher is a fifteen-second job. Azar has never done the longer task nor the simple, effortless shorter task. I know he doesn't have time in the morning to cook eggs so that's on me, the jobless wife, but out of the blue I begin to question and resent why the mundane task he surely has time for is also appointed to me.

"Are you running late?" I ask him.

"No, why?" he pours himself a glass of water.

"Aren't you going to take your plate to the dishwasher?"

Azar looks ambushed by my question, but realizing the breakfast table is five steps away from the dishwasher, he yields embarrassedly.

"I just thought you would," he quickly grabs the things, "you usually do."

Azar and I both feel the wind changing its direction. I'm shocked at what I just said after five years of not saying it. Things have changed. I have changed.

Azar acts like nothing happened and quickly changes the topic. "By the way, I'm so proud of you for helping out with the Annual Gala. I've been telling everybody my wife is planning it, so I'm hoping you girls do a good job this year."

"Don't tell people that. I'm not doing anything but making a few phone calls," I say as I realize I still haven't called any caterers. "I should probably get started on that."

"All right, you do that and I'm going to head to work now for an early coffee. I might be a bit late tonight. Big project."

Azar walks over to the table and leans in for a kiss, but I instinctively lean away from him.

"What was that?" he asks.

"I—I just don't want you to get sick."

"You're not sick anymore, you hypochondriac," he laughs and ruffles my hair like I'm a little child. "Now give me a kiss, I have to run."

I peck him on the lips and the act fills me with repulsion and self-loathing. I hate myself for showing affection to this man who's treating my emotions, my life, my future as something to be played with, disrespecting my role in his life, the sacrifices I've made for him, and my very existence. I hate myself because kissing the man I married now feels like cheating. And I hate myself for cheating on a man whose name I don't even know and who disappeared mysteriously, leaving me to long for him with an insatiable thirst.

My legs begin to shake, I crave my favourite crutch, the Red Powder. Azar leaves and I immediately heat the water for my tea and take out the Red Powder from the cupboard. Just a few months ago, I used to have to think about it—evaluate if I needed to escape reality during a very dark hour—but now I must have the powder like I need water.

The fight is no longer against a dark hour, it is about surviving a dark reality with incessant thoughts that make you want to stand at the edge of a bridge. An addict always knows they're addicted. But I will accept the lie, as if clawing onto hope with the tip of my broken fingernails, that this will be the last time before I cut down.

I stir in the Red Powder, seven good teaspoons, and impatiently wait for my tea to cool down. I have a sip, wince as the hot liquid singes my tongue, but I'm quickly satisfied with the pain. Bodily pain is the swiftest distraction from thoughts that do more harm. I close all the search pages on my phone and shake off the thoughts of the Red One, Linda, Riad, and Sonia, because these thoughts will slowly kill me.

I find the business cards Simi gave me in the bottom of my purse and get comfortable on the living-room couch. My cup of tea rests on the floor next to me as I choose a caterer to call at random. As the number gets dialed, I'm startled by a sudden knock on the door.

I assume it's my mother because nobody else is entitled enough to show up unannounced at eight in the morning. I hang up the phone and lazily drag myself out of the couch. I look through the peephole on the door to catch a glimpse of who it is on the other side.

I don't see a person but the blurred outlines of red star-like shapes. I see flowers. They're red lilies. Fiery, intensely crimson lilies.

I open the door and a stocky bearded man with a blue cap grins, "These are for Nisha."

"That's me," I nod, furrowing my brows in confusion.

The only person who would think to send me flowers would be Azar, and he knows I hate flowers. Especially lilies.

"Are you sure these are for me?" I ask the man.

He checks his tablet. "Is there more than one Nisha Abbas at this address?"

I shake my head and take the lilies. The man turns to leave when I call after him, "Who are these from?"

"Oh, I don't have that information," he says, turning around briefly, "but you might want to check the card attached!"

I feel a spark of hope that these are from the Red One. It's only wishful thinking, of course, because he wouldn't know my last name or my address. But he did say, in that honest and direct manner of his, that he would find me.

A small, folded plain white card is attached to the stem of one of the lilies. I read the printed note inside and find myself even more baffled. The note is simply an address, one I have no connection with: 124 Pinto Street.

These must be from the Red One, because there's not a single person out there who would send me an unfamiliar address. I smile with relief. The thought of never seeing him again was unbearable. I don't know how he found out where I live— maybe he's been stalking me this whole time. I'd stalk him too if I knew where to find him.

And now I do. 124 Pinto Street must be his house. I must be with him. I waste no time and chug my tea and stick the lilies into a plastic bag to throw out so Azar doesn't see them. What I'd really like to do is dry them and keep the petals hidden somewhere forever to remind me of the Red One. Maybe that's why people give each other useless flowers. The memory of receiving them far outlives their three-day beauty and inevitable burial in the compost bin. The true gift is the memory. And memories that matter never die.

I pull my greasy hair out of its ponytail and march upstairs to take a shower. I take my clothes off and step into the bathtub, coming alive as the quick stream from the showerhead washes the sweat off me. I've been nothing but a sweating and breathing corpse since that rendezvous at the motel, waiting desperately for any contact from him. Maybe I can't live without him.

I imagine being next to his naked body once again. I miss his weight on me and those strong arms that immobilize me, force me into a place of pure ecstasy. There is no worldly pain when I'm with him, because the world doesn't matter once our bodies touch.

I begin to put on my makeup in the bedroom when I hear my cellphone blaring from the downstairs couch. It's probably just Azar selfishly calling to remind me what he needs for groceries, but I wrap a towel around myself and run downstairs anyway.

I roll my eyes to find that it's just Simi calling. I let it go to voicemail, but she rudely calls again.

"Hello?" I answer as I rush back upstairs to finish dressing up.

"Hi, Nisha! How are you?"

"I'm good, just kind of in a hurry."

"Okay, I was just wondering how the catering hunt is going?"

"I have a few contenders," I lie. "I'll call you soon and let you know."

"Okay, that's great. Why don't you just bring your list to tomorrow's meeting?"

"There's a meeting tomorrow?" I ask with surprise as I sloppily brush on my foundation with one hand.

"Yes, I sent a message to the group chat and e-mailed you too?"

Simi doesn't know I haven't checked my e-mail since high school group projects and the Annual Gala group chat is on mute.

"Right, right. I'll be there for sure," I assure her so she will let me go quickly. "What time? Whose house?"

"I wrote it right there in the message," Simi laughs politely to mask her frustration. "My house, two o'clock."

I certainly applaud Simi's commitment. She's only a few months away from becoming a mother, admittedly frightened of the future, and yet she's on top of what needs to be done for this party of unabashed and blatant pretentiousness. Her reward is literally nothing but compliments on the décor and another invite from the directors to do the exact same thing next year. Maybe her motivation simply stems from the prestige of being invited again to lead—to feel needed for something other than breastmilk and diaper changes.

"I'll see you tomorrow then!" I hang up before she can say goodbye.

I park on the side of the rather unremarkable house on Pinto Street and put my sunglasses on.

This quiet uptown neighbourhood is known for its safety, its residents mostly middle-class families.

A lovely little girl in a yellow romper, maybe six or seven years of age, bounces a ball around in the driveway where a plastic basketball hoop stands. She shoots the ball with all the strength in her thin arms and misses. She tries again and again. Her brown hair shines like gold in the sunlight and I feel a twinge of sadness because I figure she must be the Red One's daughter.

If he has a daughter, there's a woman out there who's forever attached to him. She owns a piece of him forever. I don't know who she is, but I feel anger and jealousy toward her. I don't understand why the Red One would want me to come here and rub his beautiful family in my face. I don't know if he's playing some cruel mind game or there's a rationale behind my coming here.

I'm about to leave when I see the front door suddenly open and a woman's head poke out. I watch my nemesis closely. She's a light-skinned South Asian with drab, black hair, but she's too far away for me to inspect her features closely. I can't tell if she's prettier than me.

The woman appears to be yelling something to the girl and the girl yells back. They go back and forth until the little girl angrily picks up her basketball and marches inside. The woman leaves the door open, disappears shortly, then reappears and steps outside. She holds a shawl around her shoulders and walks towards the end of the driveway.

She is nothing special, I observe. Just an average face on a doughy body. She does not deserve him.

I stare at her with contempt as she proceeds to shut the gate. She notices Victoria, of course, and stops in her tracks. She walks a few steps closer out into the street to check out my car and I stare at my phone, acting like I'm here for a reason.

She's just a few metres away when I glance up at her in a most natural, unsuspicious, fleeting manner. I can see her face clearly now and immediately do a doubletake. I've seen her somewhere before. I know her.

She turns around and walks back to her house as I scan my mind for who she is. I remove the fat and age from her face and almost gasp at my realization.

It's Afreen. Riad's wife. This is Riad's house.

12

LIKE AN ANIMAL, he pees his pants and squeals wildly with fear and I, also like an animal, feel neither pity nor remorse watching him die painfully. I enjoy the long-awaited capture of my prey, so much so that I draw the knife out of him and with all my strength, stab him again and again, elevating my pleasure with every time he screams.

"Please stop!" are his last words.

"Go to hell, Riad."

His pupils dilate into deep pools of blackness and his loud breath fades as life slowly drains out of his trembling body. I remain clutching the handle of the boning knife lodged deep in his stomach and watch his dark red blood completely coat my hands.

He's sprawled on the ground between a garbage dumpster and a graffiti-covered wall. There is no light except from the moon in this part of the alley, but I can see that his face is just as ugly as I remember it. He's wearing an expensive silk shirt tucked into a pair of tailored dress pants—one would believe he was a gentleman—

My daydream is shattered by the scent of mini cinnamon

buns right below my nose.

"Nisha?" a muffled voice calls to me. "Hello?"

"Did you want one?" Simi holds out a plate of hot pastries. I shake my head and realize I'm in Simi's living room. Mariam, Jasleen, Tanzila, and Divya sit upright on the couches beside me, staring at me with their judging eyes.

"Welcome back to earth," Divya says sarcastically as the others giggle. "Did you call the caterers?"

"Yes, I did." I say flatly and hand Mariam the list in my purse.

I look at all the women in the room and realize that, except for Simi, I don't know them. One of them could be Sonia's friend for all I know. They could have found out about Riad and sent the red lilies to me to taunt me. I suspect them all.

"Wonderful."

I don't like Divya's tone. She's talking to me like she's my superior. I'd like to punch her right off her high horse and see her fall on her fat ass.

Anger has completely consumed me and now I'm marinating quietly in its belly. I'm not seething with rage. There's no steam coming out of my ears. I'm calmly angry. After seeing Riad's house yesterday, I know rage is my new normal.

All these years have inched by and I've grown more anxious, more isolated, more unhappy, and more dependent on a pointless drug—and Riad's been breathing the fresh air as free as a bird. Living with his elegant wife and beautiful daughter in a two-storey house surrounded by a colourful garden, creating memories to cherish when he's old and ready to be buried with his secrets. He's had years of joy. His life has flourished freely with not a single ripple of regret at having destroyed mine.

My cold rage intensifies when I think about his daughter. I can't forget the sight of her yesterday, running around as daintily as a ballerina in a music box. The sun shone against her small, fragile body, creating an angelic border of gold. Little girls are beauty personified; they're enchanting, innocent, simple. The unwelcome thoughts of Riad hurting her—ripping her beauty away from her like he did to me—anchor into my mind and I can't shake them away.

"I have copies here of Amatullah's latest novel—*Love in a Hateful World*," Simi says and pats an oversized twill bag by her feet. "We all need to read some of her books before meeting her. Authors can be offended by people who aren't familiar with their work. We want to show her the respect she deserves."

"Thanks, but I've already read all her stuff," Tanzila brags humbly. "I already have a list of questions I'm going to ask her."

"I've read three of her books and I'm in the middle of reading a fourth one," Jasleen boasts.

"*Love in a Hateful World?*" My voice is sarcastic.

All love eventually turns into hate anyway. You find a person you love and you relinquish your independence and marry them and then they betray you or take advantage of you or control you until the very sound of their voice makes you sick. A mother loves her baby until that baby is suddenly an adult and she is irreversibly old, left alone to resent the children who stole the possibilities of her youth only to never pick up when she calls. Even an artist who toils day and night at their beloved craft hates their passion on certain days because they're bound to it inexplicably: a forced compulsion that destroys their chance at the lazy pleasure of being popular and average. There is no love in a hateful world. There's temporary joy in hell.

"You've read the book, Nisha?" Jasleen asks, surprised, because why would a bimbo like me have the same interests as her.

"No, I just thought the title was stupid," I shrug.

The room falls silent and I can see their jaws drop.

Blurting out my unfiltered opinion feels as refreshing as chugging a cold glass of something fizzy after hours of thirst. I can't seem to hold down my words anymore for the sake of appearing civil. There are more important things—so many more important things—than what a bunch of pretentious women think about me.

"The title refers to her finding hope after a lifetime of abuse," Jasleen crosses her arms and begins her lecture. "I don't know if you're familiar with her story, Nisha, but it's one of incredible resilience. Amatullah was born in terrible conditions, surrounded by very dangerous people as a child. She experienced all types of violence and abuse but rose above it all and became one of our most celebrated authors. She's also a lecturer. She's even built several schools and orphanages for street kids—"

"How did she get out?" I interrupt Jasleen's flowery speech with a burning question.

"Get out of what?"

"How did she get out of the slums as a child prostitute?"

I don't believe angels simply grow wings and come flying out of hell. Amatullah must've been angry and is still fuming behind a smile that shrouds her darkest secrets. When you're born into pain, touched and violated, used up, beat up, hurt while the rest of the world looks away, you don't aim to be a pacifist. The chain of evil may eventually be broken but at the first link, you want revenge. You want blood.

"Well," Jasleen sighs, looks around the room, and talks to me slowly, "from what I've read, Amatullah was adopted by an American couple around the age of eleven. They found her in a girls' home, fell in love with her spoken poetry—she couldn't write until much later—and they brought her to the States with them."

"But how did she get to the girls' home?"

"We should really get back to the Annual Gala, guys," Simi chimes in and everybody except Jasleen nods.

Jasleen rolls her eyes, "Amatullah doesn't specify but I gather a missionary found her and brought her in. Why do you care? That was decades ago and irrelevant anyway. She's in her sixties now."

"Because I don't think Amatullah is as perfect as she wants her fans to think she is."

"Okay, Nisha," Jasleen raises her voice and raises her arm my way to give me the imaginary microphone, "what's your theory?"

Tanzila, Divya, Mariam, and Simi wriggle back into their seats and look at each other worriedly. This is out of everybody's comfort zone. Housewives don't argue; we smile apologetically and change the topic at the slightest hint of a conflict.

"I think she killed her pimp and ran away," I assure the wide-eyed, shocked faces before me. "Yeah, I think she cut his dick off, stabbed him in the heart and ran. She probably stabbed some perverted hobos too while she was living on the streets. I think she killed anybody who tried to touch her again until she finally made it to the girls' home, washed her hands clean, and acted like a devout Christian or Buddhist or whatever little puppet they wanted her to be. Then she charmed her way all the way to New York, taking advantage of all the connections that come with being some rich white couple's dark-skinned charity child, and told her story to make millions of dollars and fans. Hey, good for her!"

The room is so quiet I can hear everybody gulping down the heavy morsel of criticism I just fed them. Tanzila and Jasleen look especially angry. People like them, whose lives are so uneventful that their faith in humanity is only tested by the demons they read about in the news, need to worship an equal number of perceived angels to restore their dream world. People like Tanzila and Jasleen will never admit the truth that there are no angels: evil is in all of us.

"How about you just ask her yourself?" Jasleen retires into her seat, clearly fed up with me. "I'm sure she will confirm what really happened."

"No, no," Simi stops Jasleen and chuckles tensely, "you don't have to meet her, Nisha. I volunteered to drive her to the gala and once she's there, she'll be sitting at the table with our sponsors. No need to hassle her with questions."

"Yes, the last thing she needs are rude questions from people like us after a lifetime of doing good deeds," Tanzila huffs indirectly at me.

"What do you mean by 'people like us'?" I confront Tanzila.

"Yeah, what do you mean?" Divya asks indignantly.

Tanzila wipes the fake, accommodating smile off her face and starts waving her hands about nervously, "I-I mean people like us who attend fundraisers, we donate to charities—our money might help a little, but we don't really do . . . anything."

Divya scoffs and shakes her head, clearly angry with the insult. "You know, before I got married, I volunteered at a soup kitchen for the homeless. I was surrounded by drug addicts and people that smelled like pee, but I still went every single weekend to help out."

"That's amazing and I didn't mean to offend you," Tanzila backs down.

"We can't all be Amatullah," Mariam shrugs.

"Of course, we can't all be like Amatullah. Most of us aren't orphaned hippies with no responsibilities," Jasleen suddenly puts down her role model to make herself appear a little better. "You know, Amatullah doesn't even have any children."

Children become the topic now and as usual become the sole reason why nobody can get anything done. It's their children's fault they can't volunteer anymore. It's their children's fault their careers died. It's their children's fault their dreams evaporated into thin air along with their hot bodies, originality, and independent thoughts. But they wouldn't want it any other way.

They continue pretending we weren't on the brink of war just seconds ago, but I remain simmering in my thoughts. Tanzila is correct: we don't do anything. Evil dances all around us and our weapon of choice is always money. Throw enough money on a problem and hope it will one day go away—but it's never the problem that goes away, it's our guilt.

There's no amount of money I can throw on Riad's daughter to protect her from what he is doing to her or will eventually do to her. There's no way to ease the guilt. I have the choice of ignoring it all—like my mother chose to do—or I can stop it. I refuse to be like my mother.

I stand up, confident in my decision, and interrupt the unimportant chatter with a loud question: "What time do elementary schools close these days?"

They finally shut up and look up at me like I'm crazy.

"Do any of you guys know when elementary schools close?" I repeat.

"Most close at three-ish," Mariam stutters as if I'm holding a gun to her head. "Why?"

I ignore her and look at the time on my cellphone. It's about twenty minutes past two and I can probably make it to uptown before schools are dismissed and Riad's daughter is forced to go home and suffer.

"Are we done here? Do you need me for anything else?" I ask Simi.

"Well, I wanted to discuss the schedule of performances and the table layout—"

"Can you just update me with a text?"

"Um, sure."

I grab my purse and say one quick goodbye to them, feeling their disapproving eyes burning on my back. As I reach the door, I hear Simi's heavy steps behind me. I turn around to face her brooding look.

She gently grabs my shoulders and whispers, "Are you okay, Nisha? Is something wrong? You're so different lately."

"Does it matter?" I wriggle out of her grip and open the door. "Who cares?"

"I care." Simi stops whispering. "I care about you."

"Okay, so then you promise you won't tell Ikram about me running out of here today? You won't mention it to Azar next time you see him?" I test her as I step out of her house.

"Sure. If they find out, it won't be from me. Just be careful wherever you're going."

My head begins to hurt as I nearly trip over my own feet marching down Simi's driveway. The Red Powder from this morning is wearing off—it wears off much too quick lately— and I know I can't drive in this dizzy state. I turn around to find Simi watching me worriedly from her door.

"Do you really care?" I call out to her.

"Yes," she nods with insistence.

"Then bring me a tumbler with some chai and put some Red Powder in it!"

"Yes, of course," Simi looks confused by my easy request. "Three sugars, one Powder?"

"No—one sugar, three Powders!"

I wonder if there are laws against stalking a child, as I park by Beauchamp Elementary Public, the only elementary school near Riad's house, and keep my eyes on its main door. This is probably illegal, but I don't feel even a slight jolt of guilt or fear. The law isn't going to protect that sweet little girl. The law doesn't protect anybody until the damage is already done. And then it only promises a mild retribution if any.

I scan the many young faces in the crowd that's pouring out, until finally a smiling, spindly girl with chocolate brown hair skips into my view. She walks towards me with a curly-haired friend in tow, her pink backpack bouncing with every step. To think that Riad had a part in creating something so beautiful boggles my mind; the irony of such innocence being born from such evil.

The kids stare and point at Victoria as they pass by and I stay hidden behind the tinted window until Riad's daughter is just a few steps away from me. The Red Powder has given me the courage to boldly roll down the window.

"Hey, come here!" I shout.

The girl stops in her tracks and her friend glares at me suspiciously.

"We don't talk to strangers."

"I'm not a stranger," I insist. "Come closer."

The two girls refuse to step closer and stand frozen with fear and suspicion.

"I know your mother. Her name is Afreen, right?" I tell Riad's daughter and she finally relaxes her stance.

She nods and takes a few steps closer to me. Her friend holds her back, still refusing to trust me.

"I know your daddy too," I tell her. "I know him very well."

The little girl suddenly looks at me with surprise. The surprise then becomes fear and disbelief when she darts away down the street.

"You're a mean person," her friend stares at me with contempt as other children gather around to see what's going on.

"What did I say?" I ask her.

"Her daddy is dead."

13

GAUDY SILK ROSES GATHER dust in a purple-tinted plastic vase on one of the two small tables beside the ancient chestnut brown polyester couch. The other small table has an elaborate rhinestone-covered frame displaying some scripture in Arabic, which I can't read. Another large frame enclosing more scripture in gold on black hangs high above the almighty TV.

"It's so nice to have you visit." My mother beams as she brings a hot cup of chai and a coaster to the coffee table. "You should come see me more often."

I ignore her as I stare at the TV screen. One of my mother's favourite shows from back home is playing. The sappy drama is geared towards bored housewives and young girls who hope they'll never become bored housewives.

When I was little, I thought these shows from the poor old country were ridiculously unrealistic with their plots always focusing on marriage and family relations. Now I realize that these intense family dramas are far more reflective of real life than any big-budget Hollywood movies—and with more serious conflicts too. Indeed, an evil mother-in-law can be just as bad as an alien invasion. And marrying the wrong man or woman? Well, that could be the end of your world.

"This is how families should be," my mother says and plops down a few inches away from me and I move over automatically, "just visiting each other for no reason at all. I wish Tariq would come soon."

"You got rid of him," I hiss under my breath and sip the tea quickly, knowing it's burning hot.

My tongue is scorched, and I appreciate the pain that allows me temporary distraction from my mother's voice. The very sound of her voice makes my temperature rise and the words she spits out makes me clench my fists. My body is telling me that I hate her.

"I was just helping him," she chuckles innocently. "Every man has to create a life for himself. Once we find a girl for him, he will finally be married and have a successful life."

"What exactly is a successful life?" I bite back, curious if she will give me an answer that might slightly match my own view.

She looks surprised by my question. We don't do the thing known as a conversation—exchanging questions and answers, thoughts and opinions. All my life, it's just been her standing on a podium with her demands while Tariq and I cowered below her, just listening quietly because her dictatorship frightened us. Now she's old and powerless. She looks surprised and pleased to have somebody ask her for her opinion.

"A successful life is having a good job, being married, and having children," my mother states matter-of-factly.

I'm not surprised that the word *happiness* has not entered my mother's formula for a successful life. Happiness, I think, is just an afterthought for those whose countries didn't sell them a dream but rather a brutal reality: work hard if you're a man, marry up if you're a woman, or end up on the smog-filled streets with your protests. Poverty and scarcity squash that nagging voice that keeps asking you about your dreams and directs your mind to simply surviving. Wealth and excess, the way of life my generation in the West has become used to, removes the sweeping priority of survival and replaces it with a constant, excessive need for happiness and more happiness. For people like my mother, a successful life is happiness. For people like me, happiness is a successful life.

She's wrong and I'm right. I've taken her guidance and ticked off a checklist of societal expectations rooted in age, gender, and socioeconomic status. I've gone to school, I've gotten married, and I'm actively trying to get pregnant by a man who pays my bills but likes to stick his penis into twenty-something-year-olds when I'm not looking. I lead a successful life according to my mother's checklist—extremely successful—and yet I'm filled with rage and hopelessness.

My mother assures me, "Inshallah, you will have a child soon and your life will be complete."

There's so much in that sentence that angers me. She knows my life will never be "complete" because the foundation, my childhood, is fragmented by her, my father's, Riad's and Sonia's actions. She knows I was more or less sold to Azar and doesn't care how awful he truly is. She doesn't know what a joke my marriage has become—how Azar is cheating on me and I've happily cheated on him—and yet she thinks that a baby will fulfill me.

There's so much I want to shout at her right now. I could go on for hours and hours about how much she has damaged me, how much I despise her for not doing anything when I needed her the most, how much pain I still feel by her having chosen image and reputation over honesty . . . but I won't. She doesn't deserve my naked emotions and I'm not here to cry and be a victim. I will never again be a victim in yet another passive episode of self-pity.

I'm here as a predator on a mission.

I cut my eyes at my mother's hideously happy smile and ask her bluntly, "Did you know he was dead?"

My mother keeps quiet for a moment before inquiring innocently, "Who?"

She knows exactly who I'm talking about. I see it in her heavy gulp and her sudden refusal to look me in the eye.

"Riad," I say his name loud and clear.

That name has never been spoken since that night I cried in my mother's arms eighteen years ago. It was buried along with all the horrible things its owner did to me. The truth was buried. My pain was buried.

"Riad?" my mother whispers carefully, afraid to resuscitate the memory of him.

Her face is red with shame. After all these years of doing nothing but mop the floor from time to time in between chugging tea and staring at the TV—all these idle hours and days gifted by God for her to do anything she wanted—she hasn't reflected on anything in her life and hasn't evolved in her thoughts. I can see she doesn't want to continue talking about him. She's still ashamed of what happened. Does a part of her think it was my fault? She can't even stand to look at me now and I feel just as dirty as I did over half a lifetime ago.

I feel as if the word *sinner* is branded on my forehead and I should just retreat into a little corner of the world and never be seen again by all the superior, clean people. This is how I feel when my mother, whose opinion of me will unfortunately shake me long after she's dead, feels ashamed of me.

However, this time my anger is stronger and more powerful than my fear of feeling little. I allow my mother to be ashamed. I won't question her or beg her to relieve me of my guilt. I'm only here on a mission. I'm not the Nisha I used to be.

"Yes, Riad, the man who raped me." I sting my dumb mother

with the exact words. "You must've known he died. Somebody must've mentioned it to you."

My mother puts her full teacup away and nods slowly, "I knew he died."

"You knew and you didn't tell me?"

"Why do we need to discuss him, Nisha? I don't want—"

"How long have you known? How long ago did he die?"

"Three years ago."

"Three years!" I glare at my mother in disbelief. "You knew he died three years ago and you didn't bother to tell me?"

"Why do you need to know?" my mother raises her voice and crosses her arms as if to protect herself.

My anger rattles me like an earthquake and tears begin to flow uncontrollably.

"Why do I need to know? You don't think I have a right to know the guy who raped me is dead?" I spring up because I can't bear to sit next to her for another second. "You don't think he's been in my head all these years?"

"That is your problem, Nisha!" my mother points her accusatory finger at me. "You could've moved on and lived your life. You have everything—a nice house, a nice husband, money— because I forced you to forget about Riad! Why are you here to talk about him? He's dead. It's all over now."

I ignore everything she just said to preserve my sanity. She will never understand. My mother is blind although her eyes are wide open. She is not capable of empathy or sympathy. Explaining my feelings to her is just a waste of time and a major delay of my mission.

"How did he die?" I ask her calmly as I wipe away my final tears.

"He was in Europe with his father on a business trip. They rented those superfast cars to race on a track. Riad lost control of his and crashed to his death instantly. His father is still alive."

"So he died having fun?"

There's that supposed universal justice then: a man who destroyed a child died quickly racing a fancy sportscar. No life-threatening illness to cripple him with pain, fear, and sadness until his very last hour. No rotting in jail, away from everybody he loved, beaten or stabbed to death. He left peacefully, maybe only experiencing a microsecond of pain and fear, and was buried quietly with all his sins.

"He's gone now, Nisha. You don't need to think about him ever again." My mother motions for me to sit down next to her. "He will have to answer to Allah now."

I remain standing as far away from her as possible, collecting my thoughts and containing my emotions. I stare at the old carpet, the same Persian one from the old apartment, and realize my mother could move from a village to a city, a small home to a big home, one part of the world to another, and yet keep her opinions and perspectives on life completely unchanged. I wonder if it's her God that keeps her this insulated from reality or if her curiosity has completely shut down from years of being a miserable, robotic housewife.

"So, we're just going to let him get away with it? Nobody will ever know what he did?"

"Is there any point to speak ill of the dead?" My mother continues sipping her chai as if this is now a done conversation. "Allah will judge him up there. You need to find peace down here."

This has nothing to do with God. This insensitive, ignorant, selfish, evil woman who gave birth to me simply won't shut up about the imaginary judge in the sky.

"I want justice for what they did to me!" I shout at her. "I want some type of justice, don't you understand?"

She appears to be afraid of me. She knows the days of me

being afraid of her are long gone. She begs me to calm down and finish my tea.

I ask, "Where is Sonia?"

"Who?" Again she acts clueless.

"Where does she live?" I demand.

"I don't know!"

"You will tell me right now where she lives, or I promise I will tell Dad what Riad and Sonia did to me. I will call Tariq and I'll tell him everything. I will tell all your current and old friends. I'll tell Azar and even his parents. You will die of shame."

My pathetic mother fears this threat more than the fact that I'm standing right in front of her with my fists clenched.

She doesn't even hesitate to open her mouth. "I know nothing about the Khan family or any other family anymore, Nisha. I isolated myself from everybody because of what happened to you. You ruined my life that night eighteen years ago."

"I ruined your life?" I begin to laugh. My anger is so immense, it can only be expressed safely through laughter.

"You did!" my mother shouts at me. "I have nobody to talk to now. Nobody."

"You're a liar." I shake my head at her in disbelief and scorn. "How did you find out about Riad dying unless you spoke to Aunty Khan?"

"Your Aunt Nusrat told me years ago—I don't talk to her either these days. She knew somebody who knew somebody who is still close with the Khans so this could all be nonsense for all I know. Riad might be alive for all I know. Either way, it is not our business."

I reach into my purse, find my cellphone, and hold it out to my mother, "Call Aunt Nusrat right now. I have questions."

"No, I will not call her at eleven in the morning on a Jumma Friday so you can ask her strange questions. I haven't even spoken to her in years. What's gotten into you?"

I inch closer to my mother, lean over, and look deep into her eyes. "I'm not leaving until you call Aunt Nusrat."

She must know that although the woman before her may look and sound like me, there's a strange, new beast huffing and puffing that's taken over her daughter. She can feel it in her bones that I will not hesitate to hurt her to get what I want.

"Her number is in my phone," my mother shoves her cellphone into my face and looks away. "Ask her your questions and get out of my house. You've gone crazy."

I call Aunt Nusrat, whose face I can't remember at all. She was an Aunty who lived in our old apartment building and spent all her day collecting gossip to share over the telephone.

"Hello? Salam Alaikum?"

"Hi. It's Nisha. Nisha Abbas."

"Nisha? Oh hi!" She clearly doesn't remember who I am but pretends. "How are you? How is your family?"

"We're excellent." I skip all the formalities and get right to the point: "What do you know about a Sonia Khan? Where is she now?"

My mother's face is red from embarrassment as she hugs herself tightly, sitting with great tension at the edge of the couch.

"Um, well, I know of a Sonia Khan who married a dentist a while back. I've heard she still lives here in the city. She doesn't really go out to any events or weddings and hardly visits her parents. That's all I've been told of her."

"A dentist?" I chuckle sardonically. "Life is still going great for her, I see."

My mother mutters to herself, "Life is going good for you too. Try to see the bright side."

"You know nothing about me or my life," I snap at her but quickly regain my focus and stay on topic with Aunt Nusrat:

"Where in the city does she live?"

"Oh, I don't know that."

"What's the dentist's name?"

"I don't know. This is just what a friend of a friend told me. I think it was Doctor Abedin or Doctor Abdullah or something."

Satisfied with Aunt Nusrat's answers, I hang up and hand my mother's cellphone back to her. I relax my fists and move away from her. She is no longer the brick wall I tried knocking over a million times with the hope that there would be love on the other side. She is wrinkly, fragile, and vulnerable. Soon she will no longer be in this world and maybe then, during an episode of sudden amnesia stemming from the grief of my loss, I might be able to forgive her.

"What are you going to do, Nisha?" my mother asks worriedly. "Don't you hurt Sonia."

"I'm going to get justice." I chug my hot cup of tea like it's water and make my way out. "I'm going to get the justice God and you didn't give me."

I search for nirvana in a dirty motel.

I feel like I'm a teenager again, desperate for love and attention, and distracted by that constant need for love and attention. Life has come full circle. Hearing my mother's patronizing words and seeing her indifference at my pain has made me a child all over again. All my progression into adulthood—perceived progression, at least—has evaporated into the nothingness it truly had always been. I can't control the darkness inside me anymore like big girls do. I can't control my tears as I turn into the parking lot of the Bellwood Inn.

I hope to enter the reception and see the Red One sitting there just like he did that unforgettable Friday. I hope he gives me a satisfactory reason for why he disappeared on me, but my outrage would be false if he doesn't. If he wants to use my body for a brief moment of pleasure and escape, then he wants exactly what I want.

I wipe the tears and smudge eyeliner off my face before stepping out of Victoria, the only car in this quiet parking lot. Just a vision of the Red One sitting inside with his legs crossed and his deep brown eyes gazing up at me soothes all the sadness I had just felt a moment ago in my mother's living room. I swing open the reception door, my heart beating fast with hope, and see nothing but darkness and an empty couch.

The long-haired tattooed man sits on a stool in the corner, behind the glass screen of the desk. He appears to be reading something on his phone and looks at me crossly for disturbing him.

"Can I help you?" His voice is low and gruff.

He doesn't appear to recognize me, which is strange because this dead motel clearly doesn't have too many faces coming and going.

"Um," I cautiously walk closer to the uninviting man, "I'm looking for somebody."

The man scowls at me and huffs, "I can't help you with that, Ma'am."

"The guy that was here last, last Friday—the brown guy— nicely dressed, hair slicked back?"

"Oh, him?" The tension in the man's face eases and he speaks to me almost in a friendly manner, "He'll be here again soon, sweetheart. He's out on some business for a few weeks."

My desperation prompts me to brazenly ask, "Do you have his number?"

"Nobody has his number," the man chuckles.

"Thank you."

I turn around to leave, devastated that I won't be feeling the Red One's touch but elated that he hasn't left my life forever.

"Now don't go looking for him!" the man calls out after me. "Trust me, he will find you."

14

THE DATE IS the twenty-fourth of August, a date that used to pop up in my mind with positive and loving feelings. There was a routine on this date I'd follow religiously: the day would begin with me ordering warm, fluffy pancakes from a select corner in downtown and end with squeezing myself into a brand-new lingerie. But there will be none of that this year because I no longer see any importance in Azar's birthday.

However, I'm still here, all dressed up in a figure-hugging black dress with sheer arms, in this overpriced restaurant with all his friends because another year closer to his death should indeed be a celebration.

I've been running away from myself for weeks. I've been haunted by thoughts of revenge that frighten me. My mind, no matter how strongly I've tried to change its path, has been justifying a scenario of me finding Sonia and hurting her—hurting her severely.

I've searched within myself for goodness, digging through all the anger and cynicism of adulthood to find some simple moral sense instilled during childhood. I've been searching for a reason to prevent myself from doing something irreversible. I must be a completely evil woman because the only reason I mustered up is a practical and selfish one: I do not want to go to jail.

I even turned to the advice of those more worldly than me, searched the Internet for quotes on revenge by old, wise men. They say Gandhi said "an eye for an eye only ends up making the whole world blind," but he couldn't be including rape in his context of violence because rape is a special type of brutality that can't be truly reciprocated.

The rapist will always have more of the avenger than the avenger can ever take back in retribution. A rapist doesn't take your life. A rapist doesn't run off with your property. A rapist doesn't cut off your limbs so you can wear your tragedy for the whole world to see. A rapist doesn't murder your soul; a rapist grips it, controls it, dwells in it like an incurable disease until your body harbours a dark pit of worthlessness and hopelessness that you can no longer recognize yourself.

Gandhi also said, "Cowardice is impotence worse than violence." Maybe I'm just a big fat yellow-bellied coward, searching relentlessly for excuses not to hurt Sonia because I'm shaking with fear at the consequences. Jail, a completely unfamiliar territory and culture to me. It must be hell being cooped up like a helpless chicken, staring endlessly at three unmoving walls and a dozen steel bars while constantly looking over your shoulder for the most dangerous animals of all: human beings in stressful situations.

Of course, I'm terrified of spending the rest of my life in jail. And then there is the guaranteed infamy and gossip that will follow. There aren't many chai-making South Asian housewives who dabble in premeditated murder. I don't care if my mother's name gets dragged through the mud—it's the most fitting punishment for her crime—but I feel sorry that my old father will be a pariah. Azar's innocent parents will be hermits. Azar will lose all his buddies and most likely run out of Canada with his little mistress. Simi and the rest of them will pretend they never knew me and delete all photos of me smiling with them on their social media. Everybody else, neighbours, makeup clients, old acquaintances, people who greeted me at a party for a mere minute, will snicker and say, "I always knew there was something wrong with her."

Well, fuck them all and their precious reputations.

All my suffering, over eighteen years of chronic gloom and frustration under a masquerade of happiness, will be simply attributed to me being crazy. They will never understand me or even attempt to. The Khans have friends everywhere and enough money to buy respect and admiration. Few will even believe what Riad and Sonia did to me.

Indeed, taking Sonia's life would be entirely my own victory. I will be the only one celebrating behind the steel bars, unaffected by my infamous legacy and peaceful in the knowledge that justice was served. All I want is justice because justice might be the only thing to relieve me of my incessant unhappiness, but I don't know yet if being content is worth never eating shrimp cocktail on a rooftop during a hot summer day again. I still have decades of breathing to do—I don't know if I'm ready to spend them in a lonely cage. I just don't know.

"Are you looking for a new dentist?" Azar places his hand on my thigh under the table.

I pull my leg away in disgust although we just took a bunch of smiling selfies to post online. I had to wish my cheating, lying husband a happy birthday publicly of course. It's abnormal not to.

"Huh?" I look up from my cellphone.

I still have had no luck finding Sonia's husband. It appears there are a lot of dentists in town with a Muslim last name beginning with A and none of them are very active on social media. If they post pictures, it's almost always of themselves or their cottages, and not their wives.

"You're searching for dentists in the city while your salmon's getting cold. You're ignoring everybody," he whispers into my ear. "Stop being so rude."

I look around and see happy faces, over twenty of them sitting around the long table. Simi is here with Ikram. She has only said a few words to me all night. She probably broke her promise and told her husband I'm a crazy drug addict and now they're sitting together in the corner opposite from me and chatting away, obviously keeping their distance.

"What is with you lately?" Azar keeps his voice low but fails to hide the anger in his furrowed brows. "Put your phone away, eat your food fast so we can cut the fucking cake and leave."

"Why are you so eager to leave?"

"I have work tomorrow. So do most the people here. What happened to your manners?" Azar relaxes his face and looks around the table with a forced smile.

"I'm sure you'd love to be at work right now, wouldn't you?" I whisper and drop my phone into my purse to appease him. "I'll take my food to go. I have no appetite."

Azar gives up and impatiently snaps his finger at the waiter. He demands the cake be served and everybody claps in anticipation. He wraps his arm around my shoulder and, naturally, I plaster on a warm and loving smile.

The two-tier birthday cake arrives in the hands of a beautiful waitress and makes its way to the centre of the table with five other servers following. They line up at Azar's side and begin to sing "Happy Birthday . . . " when he cuts them off, "No, no, no!" and with a wave of his hand dismisses them. "My friends will do the singing."

Everybody, including the servers, take his rude behaviour for confident charm. Perhaps it is, if they think so. He is always so self-assured, the focus of admiring eyes. But if he were a woman, would he have even half as many friends as he does?

Everybody at the table stands up and begins to sing. Some take out their cellphones to record the event and post online. Azar puts on a show of a happily married guy, holding me tightly at my waist and pretending to be grateful.

"Why aren't you recording?" he whispers.

I stop singing and whisper back, "You just told me to put my phone away."

Before I can feel my cellphone at the bottom of my purse, the song is done and everybody's sitting again. They wait for the cake to be cut and served when I finally pull my phone out of my purse. A few odd things fall out and a white business card is stuck on my phone screen. It says, Dr Abrar, DDS, MSc, FRCD, orthodontist. There is an address and a phone number. Sonia's husband.

I have no idea how it could possibly have ended up here. I look around the table with the hope of catching the culprit but they are all busy chatting. It must be the same person who sent me those red lilies. Whoever it is, they know what happened to me as a child. They want me to get my well-deserved revenge.

I sip on my tea, which is mixed with a healthy dose of the Red Powder, from a plastic travel mug as I wait for the keys to my rental car. I have a cigarette in my other hand although I've never smoked before in my life. I have a red wig in my purse; my plain cotton leggings are black, my old black t-shirt has a hole in it, and my naked face is hidden behind giant bug-eye sunglasses. I am somebody else today.

The blonde-haired kid comes outside from the reception

desk to hand me the keys to the rather plain Toyota I'm rent-ing for a few days. He can't be any older than nineteen and this must be his summer job. I watch him stroll carelessly towards me in his fancy sneakers and cheap sunglasses and I envy him intensely. If only I could be him right now—a young, white male with a harmless job—I wouldn't be standing here tapping my toes with anxiety.

"Here you go, Ma'am," the boy hands me the car keys with a smile and points to the last car in a line of clean, black sedans. "My colleague is going to drive it out for you. Have a great day!"

He walks back inside, and I'm left angry and resentful at his unabashed youthful happiness. Angry because I lost that sense of optimism far too early; resentful because the world is still spinning around with people like him, happy and cheerful, when people like me are burning at the core. The world doesn't stop for anybody's pain and these smiling young people are a constant reminder of that.

An older worker parks right in front of me, his eyes fixed on me the entire time he steps out of the car. For a moment, I'm afraid he can see through me, like he knows I'm up to some-thing bad. He smiles at me flirtatiously and I remember I'm still a good-looking, normal woman on the outside, not a monster.

My legs feel leaden as I force myself into the driver's seat and place my handbag beside me. The handbag is heavy because it hides Azar's professional binoculars. They are from a trip he took to Peru with his university friends and were only for show. He has absolutely no interest in nature or birdwatching.

I wait until the man goes inside, then take the wig. The plastic cover boasts "100% INDIAN HUMAN HAIR" and I can't help but wonder which poor woman's scalp it came from. It's probably hundreds of strands from hundreds of different people. I wonder if they ever imagined their hair would be used in the West to cover up a criminal's identity.

I wrap my hair into a tight bun at my nape and slide the silky wig over my head. I like the bright red-wine-haired woman I see in the mirror. Red is danger. Red is passion. Red is fearlessness.

The woman in the mirror is not Nisha, the coward who allowed the control of her own life to slip through her fingers like soapy water. This goddess of revenge is brave, determined, and in complete control of the justice owed to her.

There's an incredible power in being anonymous. I brazenly get on the road to find Dr Abrar and follow him all the way to his home and Sonia.

I still haven't made up my mind about what exactly I will do. I've been replaying everything she did and said to me, but when judging what she deserves, I'm a hung jury. True justice would be to strip her naked, penetrate her with an object she doesn't want inside her, scar her so deeply she can't ever be normal again, laugh about it and then run away.

I'd rather just end her. I know that'd be more humane.

I turn the radio on and some beautiful love ballad blares into my ears. I turn the station to some loud and angry rap music. I don't want to hear about love, I want to hear about guns, drugs, and meaningless sex. I want all the ugliness in the world to enter me; I need the darkness to power me.

Dr Abrar's office is on the ground floor of a small office building off a busy intersection. A sign requests patients to park underground, so his car must be one of the nice ones parked in the reserved spots overground. It's a little past four, so he should be coming out anytime now. I drive to the plaza adjacent to the building and park as close as I can to get a good view of who's coming out next door.

Stalking is certainly a lot harder than what they show in the movies. In my paranoia I constantly check my mirrors, certain that somebody is following close behind me, watching me. I think every single man with dark hair leaving the office building is Sonia's husband, and then realize he's not. I found his picture on the Internet and downloaded it on my phone, and so I keep comparing the man in the photo with faces that look nothing like his. I'm unravelling and the Red Powder isn't working fast enough. But I'm already here, mentally, and there's no way to stop now.

Finally, a portly man of average height in a clean striped shirt and impeccably ironed dress pants enters my sight. He strides to his car and is the same man as in the picture but with an easy extra twenty pounds on his body. I'm surprised Sonia agreed to marry somebody like him. His wallet must be fat too.

I take a deep breath and turn the volume up on my radio. My hands tremble and my feet shake as I drive out of the plaza and follow Dr Abrar's silver Mercedes. I'm only two cars behind him when we hit our first red light. With the angry beat of rap music blaring and my forehead sweating from the heat inside my wig, I wonder what I am doing at this moment in my life. I could turn around and go home now. It's not too late to just forget this happened, with the help of more drugs and social media lobotomy.

The light turns green the moment my feet feel cold and I take it as a sign to keep going. Following Dr Abrar is easy because it's rush hour and he can't possibly notice me in the sea of cars and buses. At every red light that nagging voice in my head tells me to go home. I gulp down the tea in my mug like a parched elephant, begging the Red Powder to stifle that voice.

After what feels like an eternity on the highway, the silver Mercedes finally signals to exit. The road empties of cars and I keep a good distance behind. We drive on the local roads for another while, before I'm shocked to realize that the streets are familiar. My house is nearby and I've been driving around in a circle. All these years I thought cowardly Sonia went into hiding somewhere far away and the whole time we've been neighbours.

The silver car drives into a dainty residential street with tall houses and long driveways. There are no other cars on the street and I keep my distance. Finally I see him turn and disappear behind the garage door of a grey-brick, two-storied house. I turn the radio off.

I don't dare drive closer until many long minutes pass and my heart descends from my throat. I inch closer and closer to the dentist's house and finally park right across it, calm in the knowledge that my sunglasses and my wig have made me invisible and cocky with the bravado the Red Powder has handed me. I watch the two windows facing the street as if they were paintings at a museum. I wait for the canvas to come alive; I wait for the white curtains to draw open and reveal Sonia's face.

I take the binoculars out of my purse and adjust them to be able to see the upstairs windows closely and clearly. I rest them on my lap and watch the house without blinking. Time passes, and a few cars drive by. The sidewalks are quiet and the birds become a noticeable background. I'm finally under the spell of the Red Powder. Everything, from the grass on the dentist's lawn that moves with the wind to my cacophonic thoughts, slows down until it's all completely still and mine to control.

And then she appears from behind the curtain. I see the outline of a fair-haired woman who's not very womanly at all. She has the lithe, slim body of a teenager that she shows off in a fitted white tank top. She stretches her arms out on the windowsill and stares outside, frozen like a mannequin. I bring the binoculars up to my eyes and watch the blurry figure with awe as her facial features become distinct.

She looks the same, right down to the bleached blonde hair and the smug pout. Beautiful Sonia has remained beautiful Sonia. There's not a single wrinkle on her face or a receding hairline or any extra weight. Time has been kind to her, and karma has avoided her.

She is in a trance, staring at something ahead, arrested by her thoughts. I stare at her just as intensely as she stares at the nothingness outside. Now that I know where to find her, I wonder what I will do with her.

Maybe I should allow my anger to give my hands the strength to strangle her. Maybe I should just shoot her down like the sick dog she truly is. Or maybe I should torture her until she admits her and her brother's crime to the entire community, to my parents, and then to the police.

For a fraction of a second, she glances my way. Our eyes meet through my binoculars and although I know she can't see me and she's not looking at me, I'm as startled as a rabbit hearing a footstep in the leaves. She suddenly disappears behind the curtains and I'm left sinking into my sweat-soaked seat, containing my heavy breathing. Once again, Sonia has left me a scared, cowardly, anxious mess.

I turn the car on and blast the fan right onto my face. I need to cool down. I'm close to taking a life but it's not easy to kill. I don't know what to do next. I don't know where to start and I don't know if it might be best to just let this be the end. Maybe I'll find satisfaction tomorrow or next year or later in life, now that I know exactly where my prey was hiding, and I chose to let her go. Or maybe I won't, and her continued existence and happiness will bring me the most painful regret.

I yank the ridiculous wig off and chuck my sunglasses behind me in frustration. I cry into my hands with defeat. My face is wet with tears and sweat as the worst thought barges into my head somehow: maybe it's my life I should take. Indeed, suicide is the only flight away from this cruel mystery of an existence that nobody chose to land upon. Suicide is the only off-button to this continual state of pain: the pain of being abused, to have your humanity disregarded and reduced to your body parts; the pain of being considered far less important than the rich mortals who only own more molecules in the solid state of matter that are objects.

My quiet crying turns into sobbing when I remind myself that suicide is not the answer. There could be something much worse on the other side. This world could be the first in a series of existences, each one a hundred times worse than the last, with special punishments for those who opted out of the pain. The truth is that I don't have a solution and I still have no idea what to do with Sonia.

"God, help me," I plead between my sobs.

Suddenly, as if it were a rare answer from above, my cellphone rings.

I wipe my tears away and reach for my purse where my cellphone continues to play a heavy metal guitar riff that I don't remember setting up. The sound is harsh and violent. The caller is "UNKNOWN." I expect some telemarketer or a scammer. I decide to pick up the call anyway because I need to hear somebody's voice right now—even if it's a stranger's from across the globe.

"Hello?"

"*Come home,*" the familiar voice echoes into my ear.

"Is it you?" I ask with a smile—a smile that has forgiven and forgotten his unexplained absence.

"Yes," the Red One whispers.

"I've been missing you," I admit to him barefaced. "I've been missing you a lot."

I close my eyes and shut out the world. I just want to hear him. His voice soothes me like a sweet piano melody.

"So come home."

"Home? Where's home?"

"Your home. I'm here waiting for you." He hangs up.

I open my eyes and gasp when I see a shape in my rear-view mirror. It's him; he's right there. I turn around, but the backseat is empty.

I can no longer trust what I hear or see. Things appear real until suddenly they don't. The pharmacy, the red lilies, the business card, and now this phone conversation with the Red One who suddenly sits in my car . . . maybe, in my pursuit of escaping reality, I've overachieved.

But I head home to search for him anyway. I speed away, a slave to hope.

15

I PARK THE RENTED Toyota a few houses away from mine so I don't have to explain it to Azar. I walk towards my house looking frantically over my shoulder and in every corner of the neighbourhood for a sign of the Red One. There are no strange cars in front of my house, which hasn't been broken into. I look for nosey neighbours sitting on their patios. I feel watched—but there's nobody around. I hear faint footsteps and I turn around in circles like a madwoman, searching for my stalker. There's nobody on the street.

"Don't believe anything," I whisper to myself.

I enter my house and I know exactly where I must go. Without taking off my shoes, I make my way upstairs. My eyes catch the vacation photos of Azar and me on the wall. I pause to focus on all of them. I watch our synchronized smiles; how rigid our postures are even though we have our arms around each other; our complementing clothes that we picked out carefully months before each trip. We are a caricature. I throw my head back with a snicker that quickly rises to a crescendo of laughter. My eyes water and I hold my stomach tightly to stop it from erupting from my hilarity.

When I finally catch my breath, I find the master bedroom door wide open. I already know what I will find.

The Red One is in my bed with nothing hiding his nudity but the duvet I share with Azar. His hair is loose with no gel taming it. The scar on the right side of his neck is gone. His beautiful, chiselled face glows in the golden midafternoon sunlight and his stern eyes order me to walk closer.

I've starved for him and although I harbour a thousand questions, I just want to devour him quietly at this moment. No words are spoken before I remove all my clothes and toss them somewhere behind me. I jump on top of him, moan with relief at feeling his beautiful body again as he kisses me endlessly.

He is sweet and gentle this time. His hands feel soft, like a feather tickling my skin. I miss his strong grip because this new touch is barely there. Is he even touching me?

I pull back from our embrace and rest on his lap. I look into his eyes and there's light behind them, but they change back and forth from dark brown to black.

"Why can't I smell you?" I cry.

He ignores my question and grips my hands instead. Now I feel his touch.

"You have to get rid of her."

"Get rid of who?" I look at him with feigned shock—I know exactly who.

"When I give you the call, you go where I tell you to go."

He takes my hand and leaves a single key in my palm. It's a small silver key with no ring attached and no label engraved.

"You will need this when I call you."

16

SITTING CROSS-LEGGED ON the floor, surrounded by unassembled party-favour boxes, I toss one aside in frustration. "I'm starving. Let me order us some food."

Simi and I have finished folding some two hundred boxes and there are still over a thousand to go before we can start stuffing them with candy and teabags, gifts from the Annual Gala's sponsors. None of the other planners have shown up.

Simi looks down from the couch where she's sitting with her back awkwardly propped up against the armrest, giving the baby in her belly some room. "Do you want me to cook you some—"

"No, you're giving birth any week now. You shouldn't be standing." I find my cellphone under the piles of cardstock on the floor and decide what food to have delivered. "You know, this would've been a lot easier if Mariam and the rest of them had come to help."

"Well, it's not their fault. Priya and Tanzila had to deal with their babies and Divya had a doctor's appointment. Rabia actually got a custom-made dress for the gala and she's getting it fitted today." As always, Simi uses a flat tone with no hint of sarcasm or resentment to avoid any conflict.

I don't have a single reason left to play this politeness game. I'm going to be a murderer soon, so being perceived as belonging to Azar's circle of upstanding friends is a lost ambition. I can take off the mask now and reveal the imperfect face beneath. I can't say it doesn't feel good.

I take a sip of the laced tea Simi so politely made for me and put the cup down. She did raise her eyebrows when I shamelessly asked for twelve teaspoons of the Red Powder, but she had the sense not to question me. My stomach rumbles and Simi yawns as quietly as she can.

"Am I boring you?"

"No, Nisha, of course you are not," Simi assures me. "It's the baby. I am just so tired. I usually have a little nap around this time because the baby doesn't let me sleep at night. She's so big, I feel her every movement."

"It doesn't make you a little mad that you can't have your much-needed nap because you've been abandoned by your friends to deal with these damn boxes?"

Simi shakes her head vehemently with disagreement and laughs lightly, "That's quite dramatic. They didn't abandon me. They had things to do."

"Well, we all have things to do. Some of us just manage our time better so we can have some left to help others." I stretch my back, grab my cup of tea, and move to sit with Simi on the opposite end of the couch; a pile of finished boxes separate us. "I've ordered pizza."

"I thought you were on a strict diet?"

"No." I smile. "Not anymore."

Every meal from now until prison is not going to be analyzed for calories and fat. I will enjoy the greasiest fast foods and the sweetest desserts without hating myself. It's only a matter of time before I can no longer enjoy them.

Simi completes one last favour box before she places a hand on her obviously strained lower back. She cracks her fingers, yawns again, and finally cradles her gigantic pumpkin of a belly with both hands. She is unusually subdued today. Maybe because the baby is making her emotional or because I'm making her uncomfortable.

"Do you think they're happy?" I ask Simi and enjoy watching her squirm in her seat.

"Who?"

"Mariam, Jasleen, Divya, Tanzila, and the rest of them."

"Yes, of course they're happy. Why wouldn't they be?"

"Why would they be? How do we actually know?"

"Is it any of our business?" Simi chuckles nervously and then shrugs, "All you need to do is see the pictures on their social media. They have everything: healthy and happy kids, nice houses, good food, great vacations . . . Alhamdulillah. They are lucky."

"Yeah, everybody is happy and lucky on the Internet," I sneer. "Nobody ever snaps a picture of themselves cutting their wrist or sticking a finger down their throat so they can puke out their dinner."

Simi's lips part with shock. "Okay."

"You know I'm right."

"You are right, and I do agree with you." She appears sincere and I think her mask is finally beginning to slip. She sighs, "I don't believe anybody is happy—constantly happy, that is—but if you're less miserable than the average malcontent, then perhaps you are winning in life."

"Is this how you imagined life, Simi?" I ask her as I look around the confines of her picture-perfect living room, her domestic jail. "Is this where you wanted to be when you were dreaming about the future as a little girl? Stuck in this house, bolted down to your couch because of pregnancy, putting together a thousand favour boxes and not getting a single dollar for it?"

Simi studies me for a moment, evaluating whether my intention is to disrespect her or to simply have a rare, insightful conversation about our remarkably similar lives. She doesn't know that my intention is neither of those. This conversation is my goodbye to her. Before the deed is done and I become that hated pariah that she never knew, I'd like for her to know there was more to me than just giggles and lipstick, anger and hatred. I want her to know I was also robbed of my dreams.

"I had great ambitions as a little girl," Simi speaks softly, staring at her belly. "I wasn't a boy-crazy romantic like the popular girls or an academic slave like the nerds. I didn't want to score a perfect husband or land a high-paying, cushy job in an office. I didn't care about the usual victories of life—I just wanted to change the world for other people. I wanted to make it a better place for those who didn't have the resources to do so."

"Really? Do you really mean that?"

"Yes," Simi nods adamantly, "but people and their dreams change all the time; grand childhood visions that once seemed so vivid you could touch them evaporate into nothingness and before you know it, your only dream is to have a bigger TV than your neighbour. It happens all the time, even to the most spirited people."

For the first time, I look at Simi with admiration. "That's pretty deep."

"Thank you. I read that in one of Amatullah's books."

"What are you going to do about it?" I ask her. "What are you going to do about all the disappearing dreams?"

Simi laughs and directs me with her eyes to her pregnant belly. "I'm not going to do anything. Soon, there will be a life in my hands. Yes, this baby will rob me of a lot of time and I might never be able to pursue my old dreams again, but I want it. I've wanted this baby for a long time. I've told you I've been scared and nervous about what will happen once I have it, but there's never been any doubt of whether I wanted this baby or not."

"You're not bitter?"

"Of course, I'm not bitter." Simi smiles and I can see she's being truthful. "One dream dying doesn't mean another dream is not allowed to grow. This baby is my new dream. I have a lot of love, knowledge, and experience to give him or her. Giving birth is like immortalizing myself by writing an autobiography, but the pages aren't paper, it's the memories of my child."

I appreciate Simi's honesty and realize I've judged her too harshly. "Thank you for the conversation. We should have talked more."

"Should have?" She frowns. "Are you going to stop talking to me after the gala is done and over with?"

Well, I'd certainly be too ashamed to call her from jail.

I keep my tone warm and friendly to assure Simi that I am not offended by our inevitable parting. "Let's not pretend like we would be meeting this frequently after this thing was done. You weren't planning on calling and texting me after."

"No," Simi shakes her head convincingly, "You are wrong. I wasn't planning on our friendship being over."

I'm surprised Simi used that f-word. I didn't know we had a friendship.

I scoff, "You won't even know I'm alive after your baby is here. You'll be so busy."

"Are you not going to visit me, Nisha? You know it's normal for friends to see each other's babies?"

She uses that f-word again and I begin to get paranoid. I

wonder what her intention with someone like me truly is. I'm cold-hearted. I'm shallow. I'm a drug addict. I'm an adulteress. I'm a vault full of secrets, bolted up and made with reinforced concrete. Nobody wants to be my friend.

She must know something; it finally dawns on me. She's not who she says she is.

I push away all the silver boxes between us so they fall to the floor and lean into her, "Are you the one leaving those bread-crumbs around?"

"What?"

"Is it you, Simi? Did you send me those lilies with Riad's address?"

"I don't know what you're talking about." Simi moves back from me, protecting her stomach with her hands.

I glare at her and demand, "What do you know about me, Simi? Why do you want to be my friend so badly?"

Simi wipes the beads of sweat from her forehead, points to the scarlet cup in my hand, "B-b-because of that."

I'm reminded of what's in my system. I force myself to retreat from a fearful Simi. I curl up against the opposite arm-rest with my feet up, hugging myself to avoid my hands from doing something I might regret. We watch each other for a long moment.

Simi finally breaks the silence. "I-I've been there, Nisha."

I keep quiet and let her talk. I can't trust myself in this state.

"I used to be like you," Simi removes her hands from her belly, disarming herself. "I used to be an addict."

"You?" I hoot at her outrageous confession. "You're lying."

"No, I am not." Simi sits closer to me so I can witness the conviction in her eyes. "I used to drink the Red Powder every single morning, afternoon, and night. I used to drink until I blacked out. I used to snort coke every weekend at the clubs."

"You? Ikram's wife? Ikram—the guy who hasn't missed Friday prayers since elementary school—did coke at a haram club? Ikram would never—"

"Ikram is Ikram," an irritated Simi interrupts. "He doesn't know about my past."

I gawk at the alien before me. All my previous convictions about Simi are in a whirlpool in my head. She has flicked the light off the halo I always envisioned on top of her head and here she sits, a person with flaws and trails of darkness.

"I'm hoping you won't tell Azar about this?" Simi says. "I've never told anybody but my sister."

I won't betray her trust. She has handed me something sacred, one of her deepest secrets. It's an act of courage to reveal your sins to a fellow member in a community that derives entertainment and superiority from judging you. It's an act of selflessness to admit your failings to make someone else with the same failings not feel alone. It's an act of friendship.

"My lips are sealed," I promise, still shaken.

"You need to quit, Nisha. You need to stop before it gets worse." Simi places her hands firmly on my knees, her round eyes piercing into mine with her warning. "I know the Red Powder is the hardest to quit because it seems so innocent—hey, our Aunties and Uncles have it all the time so it can't be that bad, right? They approve of it, and they always know what's best, right?"

"I appreciate you telling me about your past, but you don't need to worry about me, Simi. I can quit it anytime."

"No, you can't." Simi shakes her head disapprovingly at my lie. "It's not the drug you are addicted to, it's the peace it gives you from whatever you're running from. You're going to use more and more so you can keep running, and then one day you'll use so much you'll be too far gone."

"I'll be fine, Simi—"

"I ended up in the hospital once after a bad trip—I had no idea what was real and what wasn't. I did something bad—really, really bad—and I had no memory of it at all. That's the night I confessed everything to my sister and she got me professional help. I know the right people. I can help you."

"I don't want any help—"

"You need help. You need to face, accept and heal from whatever it is you're running away from. Nisha, what are you running away from?"

I feel a sudden and powerful wave of anxiety. The room begins to spin. I hold my head with both hands as if to keep my balance. I'm taken back to age thirteen, back to my old bedroom, just moments before I told my mother about Riad. Nauseated and afraid, I turn away from Simi's concerned gaze.

"Nothing," I say, not looking at her. "My life has been perfect."

Simi gently touches my chin and turns my face towards her. Our eyes lock and I begin to cry.

I can't stop crying when she comes over to me and hugs me with protective arms. She pulls my head into her chest, not caring that my eyeliner and mascara seep into her white shirt. I feel her pregnant belly against my body. I feel her baby kick while she taps my back gently.

"I'm dealing with it," I say through my sobs. "I'm dealing with it my own way."

"All right," she says, "I'll be here when you're done. I'll be here."

17

IT'S GALA NIGHT, and I try to rediscover the joy in painting my face.

Beautifying myself daily was not just the fine print in my marriage contract—I did genuinely enjoy it and treated it as an artistic endeavour. I used to equate my bare face to a canvas and my tableful of makeup to a painter's palette. But it turned into empty, unpaid work.

Azar waltzes in and out of our bedroom. I can see his reflection in the vanity mirror, peeking my way constantly, evaluating how I look. He is wearing a navy silk shirt under a dark grey suit. I refused to pick it up from the dry cleaners earlier. He ended up going himself and I think both of us are impressed he completed the task without getting lost.

We are drinking wine because an event as pretentious as the Annual Gala requires us to. Azar is sipping slowly from his glass. I'm gulping mine down. My wine, of course, is mixed with the Red Powder.

"You should wear a lighter shade of lipstick." Azar stares at my reflection in the mirror. "Red makes you look old."

I look at myself in the mirror with him standing behind me.

I study the reflection of us: he in his typical suit and I in my raven saree with a royal purple border glittering with sophisticated golden beadwork. He looks good. I look great.

"I like the red," I declare as I finish my upper lip and smack my lips together with satisfaction.

"Take it off," he demands. "It ages you. Only fat, retired Aunties wear red lipstick. They can't get attention any other way."

"You know," I turn away from the mirror, short on patience, and look at my husband who isn't expecting a retort, "one day I will be old. And so will you. What will you do then?"

Azar takes his time to think of what to say.

"I will take you out for dinner and you can wear the brightest, tackiest red lipstick you want."

"Are you sure you wouldn't just find somebody younger?"

"You're ridiculous, Nisha." Azar turns his back to me dismissively, adjusting his shirt cuffs as he walks away towards our bed.

He takes his jacket off and puts it down, not caring that I'm still waiting for an answer to my question. He finds two ties and holds them up against his shirt.

"Silver or checkered?" he asks.

"You didn't answer my question," I snap.

He rolls his eyes and grumpily puts his ties down before sighing, "What did you say, Nisha?"

"I asked . . . " I pause as I force myself to ignore the messages of a naked Linda, "will you find somebody younger when I get old? Are you going to cheat on me?"

"I would never cheat on my wife," Azar asserts without a tinge of shame, guilt, or regret on his face.

"Really? You wouldn't dangle your money and your car to some pretty intern with dollar signs in her eyes? Enjoy her body, satisfy your endless lust while thinking it's okay because I'm at home with my cane and my dentures, not having a clue about it?"

"Nope. I would never cheat on my wife."

I watch him choose the silver tie and play around with his collar. My words have just rolled off his shoulders. Maybe he heard me loud and clear—and knows that I'm talking about Linda—but doesn't care.

I put down my makeup brush and turn away from the mirror towards him. "You've never checked out any of the girls at work?"

Azar cuts his eyes at me cockily and laughs, "You're escalating this a little too fast, no?"

He turns his back to me again and I become hot with anger. I'm sitting here with rollers tugging at the roots of my hair and thick goo all over my face for nothing. All of this is a waste of time. All this glamourizing and grooming, preening and posing, is all to make this man look good and this man could not care less about me. This whole marriage is a lie, a show to mimic something ideal with the hope of feeling normal. I am not normal. I don't know any more why I'm still here.

"Who do you think I am?" I demand. "Do you think I'm blind? Do you think I'm dumb?"

"What are you going on and on about?" Azar shouts at me. "Did you call that damn doctor I told you to see?"

"I don't need a shrink!" I force my tears back. "I need honesty. I need truth."

I know my thoughts are reflected in my glossy eyes and he can peer right into them. Right at this moment, he must know that I know about Linda.

Azar sits at the corner of our bed and pats his thighs pensively. I don't expect him to crawl on all fours and beg me for forgiveness, but I wish to see just a flash of remorse in his eyes. I don't care if his guilt is based on love; I just want to know if all these years of shutting myself indoors, taking care of his meals and washing his clothes, has earned me and my feelings any importance to him at all.

Azar takes a deep breath and looks me right in the eye. "The truth is that we have a big party to attend and everybody we know is going to be there along with a bunch of especially important people who are much, much bigger than you and I. I have a reputation, Nisha. People know me and they have expectations of me. We don't need to advertise our problems and nobody needs to know my wife is crazy."

"Why do you only care about what other people see?" The tears sting my eyes with runny mascara. I have never yelled at Azar—not even once in our five years of marriage—for fear of his red-hot temper, but suddenly I'm brave. I spring up from my chair and roar at him, "What about us? What about what you have done?"

"Sit down, Nisha!" he commands me like a dog. "I have made stupid mistakes and I'm willing to talk to you about them, but we will do that later, after the gala."

I refuse to sit down. "That's what you call sleeping with some girl at work? A stupid mistake?"

"We will discuss it later tonight, after the gala."

In a whirlwind of anger, I grab one of my makeup brushes and hurl it at him, just barely missing his forehead. "I want to discuss it now!"

Here we are, Azar and Nisha, the perfect couple who married out of true love, breathing heavily and staring each other down like two tigers battling for territory.

Azar's eyes enlarge as he jumps up from the bed, dashes towards me, and grips my right forearm with the strength of an eagle's talon. I try to twist away and accidently knock over the glass of wine from the vanity with my other arm. The glass shatters violently as Azar twists my forearm with such might I cry out in pain and beg him to let go.

"Don't you ever yell at me like that," he growls at me, gripping my arm. He rips the loose end of my saree off my shoulder, leaving me with my stomach exposed. "Everything you have is because of me! I paid for this saree and all that colourful shit on your face! Don't you forget! You would be nothing without me!"

"Let me go," I beg him through sobs, pulling my arm away fruitlessly. "I'm sorry I yelled."

Azar loosens his grip and curls his lips at me with disgust. He paces around the room, gathers his composure, and fixes his hair. I sit back into the chair in front of the vanity, as deep as I can, like a frightened animal shivering at the back of a cage. My saree slips off me, the heaviness of the rhinestones pulling apart the pleats. I shudder in my dull beige underskirt, staring listlessly at the bejewelled silk on the floor and the broken glass shining beside it.

"Put your saree back on," Azar gestures with his stern finger. "I'm sorry about grabbing you like that. I just want tonight to go smoothly."

"Okay."

"Fix your makeup. Take the rollers out of your hair. Let's just go and have a good time."

"Okay."

This is the only way to keep Azar happy. I must comply. I must shut up and comply.

Azar steps closer to me and I'm afraid of what he will do next. I'm afraid he'll grab me again or kiss me as if everything is simply fine. Either action—any action from this brutish, selfish, egoistic man—will force me to do something I might regret. I want to tell him about the Red One. I want to hurt him.

He bends down and begins to put aside the larger pieces of broken glass. "Look what you did, Nisha. Tonight was supposed to be fun and romantic."

"I . . . " I pause and think of any way in which I can find the strength to stop myself from speaking. I fail. "I made a simple mistake too, Azar."

"What?" he looks up. "What mistake?"

A loud ding from my cellphone pries my eyes away from him. I check my phone to see a new message alert from an unknown number.

"What mistake, Nisha?" Azar charges me with a bewildered look upon his face that resembles a man who just got robbed of his life savings.

The message reads: "Get in your car. It's time."

It's the Red One, my true love. My one and only love. The man I want to give all the time I have left on this planet. Everything and everyone else is a complete waste of time, including this marital soap opera.

"I have to go right now." I spring up and clumsily wrap the saree around myself.

"Go where? The gala is in less than two hours!"

"It's Simi. She needs help at the hall."

"Are you lying to me?" Azar looks like the angry, betrayed spouse now.

"I'll meet you there." I quickly swipe eyeliner on and pat some blush on my tear-soaked cheeks. "I don't think they want anybody but the organizers there yet."

"Where the hell are you actually going?" Azar points an accusatory finger at me. "You still have curlers in your hair."

"I'll take them off in the car."

I throw all my jewellery and makeup into my purse, force my

feet into my heels and find a water bottle in one of the vanity drawers. The water is mixed with a dangerous amount of the Red Powder, an amount equal to the pure pill. I don't remember when, but I left it there in case of an emergency—an evening like this when I didn't just long for a temporary distraction, but a complete getaway from this planet.

"You're not going anywhere without telling me about your stupid mistake." Azar places himself in front of me.

"All these days of coming home late and now you're suddenly interested in me? You want to know my stupid mistake, Azar? This is my stupid mistake!" I shove the bottle into his face before I open the cap and gulp down the water. "It's twenty teaspoons of the Red Powder. Very potent. Maybe enough to make me crazy."

"You're already crazy." Azar coldly returns to his glass of wine.

I leap into the rental car, buckle my seatbelt with trembling hands and reply to the text message. I receive the simple instruction: "Straight, left, left, right, left."

The sun has begun to set and the pink and lavender sky looks like an abstract painting. The floating clouds have eyes and they're watching me drive with one hand and use the other to tug at the rollers in my hair. I pull them off one by one, numb to the pain on my scalp because the Red Powder has taken me over. I glance at myself in the rear-view mirror and see something resembling a pretty clown. My saree hangs clumsily off my shoulder, my makeup is blotchy where the tears flowed, and my curls levitate in all directions. What a great look for the most passionate night of the year.

I've driven according to the Red One's instructions, which have led me to a deserted road. Strangely, I don't know where

I'm going but every tree and every turn on this street appears familiar. I would have lazily dismissed it as déjà vu, but I trust my instincts and drive slower for a moment, trying to decipher this familiarity. I know this place.

The daylight is gone now and I drive towards the dark blue horizon surrounded by nothing but the silhouettes of trees. The car begins to beep to tell me I'm running low on gas when I realize there are no people or houses or even streetlights around. I could turn back and rush to the safety of a gas station, but for some reason, I know exactly where I need to go and I need to be there as soon as possible.

I already know what will show itself at the next turn, but I am still in awe when I see it. A store with a small parking lot presents itself to my left. It's the pharmacy. But this time there is no red sign or clear windows. It's a store in the middle of nowhere with a FOR LEASE sign glued to its opaque door and all its windows have been obscured with pages from newspapers. Just as I had imagined.

I park close to the store entrance and gloss over the newspaper articles, gulping heavily as I recognize all their stories. All the murdered women, kidnapped children, and corrupt politicians were in the news two years ago. The pharmacy never existed.

The Red One wanted me to come here for a reason. I grab my purse and find the rusty key he gave me in my wallet. I step out of the car, clutching the pleats of my saree in anticipation of what's inside the store. I know this key will open its door.

The key clicks into the keyhole with ease and I breathe with both fear and curiosity of what's on the other side. Before I open the door wide, I look over my shoulders to see if anybody is watching me in the dark. I wish the Red One was somewhere nearby. He promised all my problems would be solved once I answered his call. I wish he would just pick me up in his car and drive me out of this stale city tonight.

I open the door and find myself standing in complete darkness. The door suddenly shuts behind me and I begin to paw at the wall to find a light switch. I fail and reach into my purse to find my cellphone for its flashlight. Just as I recognize the cold feel of my phone, I'm startled by a muffled moan.

"Who's there?" I call out, my fists clenched, ready to defend myself.

I quickly turn the flashlight on and point it frenziedly in every direction. Every illuminated corner is just a blurry wall with cracked white paint until I see what's straight ahead of me. I jump back at the sight of a bruised body in a black bra and panties on a chair and bloodied feet tied together at the ankles with a thick tweed rope.

"Oh God!" I gasp as I shine the light on the terrified eyes before me, "Oh my God!"

A near naked Sonia leans over listlessly on the chair, her hands pulled back and bound together behind her. Her mouth is covered with a piece of duct tape. Her bleached hair has matted into something resembling a bird's nest and her eyes appear dark and puffy from a beating.

There's an old brass floor lamp beside her with a dirty, yellowed lampshade, the kind my parents had in our old apartment. I hastily plug it into the wall.

Her muffled cries make my spine tingle.

"What happened? Who did this to you?" I carefully pull the duct tape off her mouth and stare at all the scratches on her face.

Sonia coughs and gasps and finally exhales and shrieks at the top of her lungs, "Help! Somebody help!"

Driven by panic, I try to force the duct tape back over her mouth, but she throws her head from side to side and continues screeching for help. I grab a chunk of her hair to keep her head steady and ferociously slam the duct tape on her lips. The sheer strength of my violence stuns me.

My body and voice shakes as I plead with her, "Please stop screaming. I'll take this off if you don't scream. Promise you won't scream? Sonia, promise?"

She nods, and I carefully take off the tape.

"Who did this to you?"

She looks up at me, her eyes wide with horror, as she utters quietly, "You're a fucking psychopath."

"What?" I shake my head in absolute denial. "I-I just got here. I didn't do this, Sonia."

"You did this," she nods with her daring eyes before her hushed voice explodes into a cry, "You did this!"

"No," I plead with her to believe me. "I would never have done this."

"Now you have amnesia? I've been here for almost two days now, pissing myself and drinking my own spit, you bitch. Let me go!"

I watch the bruised woman before me squirm desperately for freedom. She's being violated by my eyes watching her near nudity; she is powerless with her hands and feet tied. Sonia is finally me nineteen years ago. I've fantasized about her feeling this exact pain for years, but I don't feel vindicated by this reality. I still see her as strong and invincible and so—even when beaten and stripped—she wins.

I look at the state of her ankles, covered with scabs and fresh blood from where the rope has continuously cut her. I bend down to untie her but my hands tremble so violently that I can hardly grip the rope. I'm nauseous by the stench of her urine when I notice the older blood and cuts between her thighs.

"Oh my God, I'm going to get you free and I'm gonna call an ambulance."

"Yeah, call the police too, you bitch." Sonia spits at me and springs up from the chair, only to be thrown back in by her bound hands.

I wipe her spit off my forehead and grit my teeth. "I didn't do this, Sonia. Believe me, I wanted to, but I didn't do it."

Or maybe I did.

In the low light, I notice a slight red mark on the side of my left hand. I hadn't noticed it all earlier today. I rub it vigorously, but it refuses to go away. I look at my right hand now, and two more scratches glare back at me with accusation.

The drive down the road here felt far too familiar to be insignificant. But I can't remember anything at all. Indeed, I have no significant memories from the last two days. All I remember is drinking the Red Powder from morning until night.

I try again to untie Sonia's ankles, but the knot is impossibly tight. The one at her knees is looser and I'm able to get it off. I rush behind the chair to assess her wrists when she begins to laugh at me.

She turns her head slowly behind her, looks right at me, and grins with a gleam in her eyes. "I'm glad my brother did what he did to you."

Her words blindside me like a punch and I freeze.

"Did you hear me? I'm glad he raped you."

I begin to gain control of my shaking fingers and racing heartbeat. The more the anger in me builds, the less worried and sympathetic I feel towards her.

"You should really shut up," I warn her.

"Don't you wanna know why I'm glad?"

"Just shut up."

I avert my eyes because I can't stand to look at her. My hands refuse to help her.

She doesn't speak until I lock eyes with her again. She smirks in the exact same callous way she used to smirk when she saw me in Riad's room. "You deserved it."

"Shut up," I say as quietly and controlled as I can. It is only because of the Red Powder's power to calm me that I don't break apart in tears.

"You were always acting so innocent, but deep down you wanted it. You had no shame then and you have no shame now."

"You're still tied to this chair," I remind her as she fixes her cruel, empty eyes on me. "You're trapped here with me. I can finish you right now—"

"You grew up with nothing. You wanted to be like us. You kept coming to my house with your desperate mom and your fat brother, always wanting food and gifts. You kept eyeing all my things, kept sucking up to my mom, you dreamt about marrying Riad one day."

I step in front of her again and ask her one last time, "Please shut up, Sonia."

"You ask why I never stopped my brother?" Sonia leans into me as far as she can. "It's because I know you wanted him to fuck you."

I smack her smug face with all the might of my hand. The slap booms throughout the empty room along with her scream. I've never laid a hand or even thrown the smallest of rocks at another human being and now I realize I've missed out on something. Few things have felt better than smacking the smugness off Sonia's face. I slap her again. And again. And now I'm the one smiling.

"I'm glad Riad used you like the slut you are!" Sonia howls at me through sobs.

"Sonia," I wipe her tears away and announce to her regretfully, "I think I'm going to kill you tonight."

She puts her head down, gathers her thoughts, and dares to

laugh at me again. "You don't have the guts."

I wish she were right. I'm prepared to wrap my hands around her neck and squeeze her out along with all the memories that don't leave me be. I know where to dump her lifeless body too. I don't know how I know, but I know there's a park that leads into the woods not too far from here.

I place a palm on the right side of her neck. She twists her body and face about, trying to escape my clutch. I feel her skin and the bone beneath it. It's funny how our necks are so soft and yet so hard at the same time. I wonder how tight I need to squeeze.

I place my other hand around the left side of her neck. She doesn't move her eyes away from mine as if to show me her humanity and plead with it for her life. I don't see anything in her eyes except the familiar fear of a twelve-year-old me. This is the fear of having your body under the complete control of somebody else. This is the fear of expecting pain and not knowing how much of it is coming.

I am so satisfied by watching her fear that I squeeze her neck harder and harder. I squeeze as hard as my strength allows me until I'm startled by the ringing of my cellphone.

I let go of Sonia, who exhales with relief. I check my phone to find out it's Simi calling. I'm immediately reminded of the gala and how late I am. I need to decide, right now, how tonight will end. I ignore the call but the phone keeps ringing like an urging siren.

"Not a single word or I swear I'll hurt you." I quickly put the duct tape over Sonia's mouth again. She moans loudly in protest and I roughly kick her shin to shut her up.

I control my nerves and force my voice to stop shaking. I take a deep breath and answer the phone as normally as possible, "Hi-hi Simi? What's up?"

"Hi Nisha, how are you?" Simi blurts out.

"Um, good. Just driving—um, on my way to the gala," I wince with guilt as I lie to my only friend in the world, but it's not like I can tell her I'm in the middle of an attempted murder. "Are you already there?"

"No, I'm not. I'm about to give birth."

"What? Oh my God, I'm so excited, but isn't it early?"

I find myself smiling with genuine happiness and anticipation, even with all the stress and tension knotting up my stomach and hammering my head. My joy is disrupted by Sonia bouncing around in her chair, desperate to grab the attention of whoever is on my phone line. Luckily, Simi is too anxious to hear the thuds.

"My water broke and we're driving to the hospital," Simi pants and speaks so quickly her words run into each other. "I'm obviously not coming tonight so I need a huge favour from you."

"Sure, anything. What can I do?"

"Are you driving Victoria—the fancy car?"

"Um, yeah," I lie again.

"Perfect. I need you to pick up Amatullah from her hotel. You cannot be late."

"What? Why? Why can't she just grab a cab?"

"That would be an insult. We promised to pick her up."

"Simi, I'm, um, very busy right now. Can you call somebody else—"

"You just said you're on the road. Just do a quick detour. I'll let the others know you'll be late because you're getting her."

"No, wait a minute—"

"Oh my God!" Simi cries out and I can hear a panicky Ikram urging her to hang up.

"Are you okay?"

"Contractions," she dismisses the pain and continues with heavy breaths, "you must pretend like you've read all her books. She hates people who aren't familiar with her work. We can't insult her."

"But I haven't read a single one of her—"

"Thanks a million, Nisha. I knew I could count on you. You're a real friend."

I sigh defeatedly. "Okay. I'll get her."

"I'll text you the hotel's address. Get her right now. Bye!"

Simi hangs up and I return to face this tied-up, duct-taped, half-naked woman in the chair.

Panic crawls up my body as I pace back and forth, desperate for a plan. I wonder where the Red One is now. He's vanished again, abandoned me just when I need him. Only he could give me the strength to finish this job, get rid of this creature called Sonia.

The Red Powder has begun to abandon me. I forget the overwhelming pleasure I was having strangling Sonia and begin to obsess over how easily I could get caught. Any idiot right out of police school could prove I was here. My fingerprints are all over the rope, the duct tape, the door handle, the chair. My hair strands could be found on her. The beads from my saree could be all over the floor.

I can't risk being found here so I pull her arms up and wiggle her out of the chair. She stands up now but is barely able to walk. Her head begins to hang forward and her mutters suddenly weaken.

"You will get into my trunk," I tell her firmly and push her towards the door.

Sonia's eyes are barely open as she begins to move.

"We're gonna go pick up a celebrity," I talk to myself, "and then I'm gonna get rid of you."

18

I DON'T HAVE ENOUGH gas to make it to the airport hotel where Amatullah is staying. I'll have to drive her to the venue anyway. My radio is near maximum volume because I can't stand the thought of hearing any sound from Sonia. I don't know if she is even making any sound. Maybe she has decided to stop fighting and accept her fate. Maybe she has suffocated, I will be found out, and my life as I know it has ended tonight. Either way, an upbeat country song is helping me drive in a straight line.

I see a gas station near a large intersection and decide to pass because it's far too busy. I drive towards my house where there's another, smaller station. I'm very tight on time and I can almost hear Simi's voice in my head telling me how important it is not to insult Amatullah, the world-renowned author, the international role model, the survivor, the healer. Luckily, the small gas station near my house is empty of cars. The only person around is the attendant inside the kiosk and he is busy looking at his phone.

I grab my wallet and turn the car off. The radio shuts off and I listen carefully to the silence punctuated by the sound of the occasional car racing by outside. There are no muffled screams. There is no scratching or hitting on metal. It is safe now to enter the world outside.

I step out, wrap my saree properly around my shoulders and walk slowly over to a gas pump. It is a cool late summer evening. I insert the gas nozzle into the tank opening and keep a keen eye on the attendant and a sharp ear out for any sound from the car. Every streetlight feels like a spotlight over my head.

When the gas tank is full and paid for, I hurry back to the car, nearly slamming my head as I get in. The attendant looks up from his phone—and I'm startled and stare back at him with my eyes wide open. After a few long awkward seconds of us staring at each other, he smiles flirtatiously and waves.

I turn the radio back on and zoom off to the airport. Just being locked in this car with Sonia's body, dead or alive, unnerves me and my stomach is tight with pain. I don't know if this deep, cramping pain is guilt. I haven't admitted to myself, yet, that I might have taken a life.

I look at my hands and imagine the scratches now on them morph into streaks of blood. I slow down and watch the airplanes taking off into the sky, flying up and away from all the catastrophes on the ground. The image of people flying away to wherever they want brings tears to my eyes. I'll never enjoy my freedom again.

I pull into the driveway of Amatullah's hotel. Limousines and cabs are lined up at the main entrance. The doormen are busy attending to the well-dressed guests. I take a deep breath and get behind one of the cabs before texting the number Simi sent me earlier. Amatullah will probably be appalled that her chariot of the night is not a limousine but some dirty, cheap Toyota.

A woman in her sixties in a red blazer over a long black silk dress that falls to her ankles steps out of the hotel lobby and into my view. As she comes closer, I notice she is wearing stylish black gloves to cover her hands. You would have to be somebody famous to be wearing an outfit this pretentious. Her salt-and-pepper curls fall to her shoulders and blow slightly in the wind. It is not until she is beside me at the passenger door that I realize she looks familiar. I know I have seen her somewhere before.

I pay attention one last time to the back of the car to make sure Sonia is quiet. My legs shake as I roll down the window and release some of the boiling tension inside this car out into the world. I step out of the car to greet the elegant woman.

She appraises the car and my appearance with a critical eye before shaking my hand with a firm grip.

"Hello, are you Simi?" She has a very slight British accent.

I open the door for her and say, "N-n-no, I'm, um, Nisha. Simi is actually, um, giving birth as we speak. Nice to meet you."

"Wow. All right then," she says and gets into the car. I go over to the driver's side.

"I am Amatullah by the way," she says.

"Yes, who doesn't know who you are?" I give a nervous laugh.

I'm struck by her perfume. The scent takes me back to an almost dead memory of rolling down leafy, emerald hills with Tariq. This stranger reminds me of playing with my brother in the summer, licking all the melting ice cream off our fingers, and boasting about grand dreams.

I take in her features and continue to wonder where we could have met. The colour of her eyes, a jade green inside a ring of brown, stands out against her dark olive complexion. She has a small pointy nose, high cheekbones, and slight lips brazenly coloured in scarlet lipstick. I imagine she was quite beautiful in her youth. She is quite beautiful now.

She looks at me looking at her then cuts her eyes to her dazzling wristwatch. "We are late to this gala of yours."

"Yes, I sincerely apologize."

We emerge from the hotel driveway and I don't know whether I should turn the radio on. While I need to blast the music to drown out Sonia, I don't dare offend Amatullah. She may be a petite lady but she is intimidating.

"W-would you like music?" I bravely ask.

"No, thanks." She smiles. "A good conversation is the only melody I like."

I realize I'll just have to talk continuously and loudly for this entire twenty-minute ride. "So how do you like Toronto?"

"Toronto . . . " she sighs, "it is a special Rubik's Cube."

"How so?"

"You see all the colourful squares scattered around each other, living in peace as neighbours, serving a function and being handled and pivoted easily by those who want them in line. But to solve the puzzle, to have six solid facets and still serve one common goal, is the difficult part."

"You mean to stand with your own colour and still be a part of the whole cube?"

"Yes, exactly. Whenever I come to this city, I feel a terrible sense of inauthenticity in its people. People will say things, do things, condone things that are in direct opposition to their true selves—mostly for simple acceptance. It must get lonely in this big city."

"So, you think Torontonians are fake? I disagree. Phoniness exists in every city. It's everywhere. It's human nature to be something you're not if it benefits you."

"Perhaps," Amatullah says, "maybe that is why most Rubik's

Cubes end up gathering dust somewhere before the puzzle is ever solved."

I chuckle in agreement as we stop at a red light. I watch Amatullah's bright face in the streetlights, wondering again where I have met her.

She catches me staring at her. "Is everything all right with you, dear?"

"Sorry, I just feel like I've seen you before."

"Of course, you have seen me before!" Amatullah laughs. "My face has been plastered all over your bookstores. I have been on your television screen a hundred times."

"No, I feel like we have met before. I feel like we've chatted before."

"Yes, maybe." Amatullah takes a long look at me. "We probably have in a previous life or in another dimension. Maybe we are both the same recycled soul, split into two different bodies and experiencing two different generations at the same time."

I try my best not to make a patronizing face. "You believe in that stuff?"

"I believe in all kinds of stuff. I believe everything and anything is possible. Have you not read my books?"

I gulp heavily as I remember what Simi and the other planners told me about Amatullah's dislike of people who haven't read her books. I don't want to anger this woman—not because her elegant way of speaking and lovely perfume has already impressed me, but because I genuinely like her. I feel an inexplicable closeness with her.

"I'll be honest with you," I tell her with my head lowered with regret. "I haven't read any of your books. I looked you up online though and I read a lot about your life."

I expect to see steam blowing out of Amatullah's ears but instead I see an indifferent shrug.

"I don't blame you, my dear. My life is a lot more interesting than my ramblings."

I breathe out with relief. I tell her, "You're not what I thought you'd be like."

"Oh, really? What did you think I would be like? An angry old lady driven to madness by writers' block and disgruntled at pretty young ladies like you?"

"No," I chuckle. "They made it sound like you were unapproachable. You know, unfriendly. But you seem so . . . cheery."

"Well, I certainly do not like being approached and I have very few friends," Amatullah agrees, "but I have always liked cheering up the malcontent and sombre."

"Are you talking about me?"

"Yes."

I don't know whether to be offended or not. "What makes you think I'm those things? Malcontent and sombre?"

"Well, my dear, your makeup did not swim by itself all over your visage. You tried to cover it up with that fresh eyeliner, but your puffy eyes reveal that you have been crying. You have cried a lot. And that beautiful saree? One does not wear such a spectacular and expensive fabric so clumsily if everything is all right in their universe. Or at least bearable."

"Oh, you're talking about my appearance." I completely forgot how disheveled I look. "I'm fine. Just had a fight with somebody."

"I did not ask if you were fine."

"Okay, then," I'm taken aback by her rude reply. "I guess I'll just be quiet until we get to the banquet hall."

Amatullah doesn't apologize for her abruptness but instead rolls her window halfway down and breathes in the crisp evening air. She stares bright-eyed at the streets and buildings and lights of the city as if they were magical. All I see is dull cement and brick.

We are just about ten minutes away from the hall when she rolls up her window and speaks into her lap in a soft tone. "Pain is just a normal part of existence. The beauty of it is quite overlooked and dangerously underrated."

"The beauty of pain?" I scoff. "That's very poetic but I don't think it makes a lot of sense."

"Of course it does. Define beauty for me, Nisha."

"When something looks pretty or makes you feel nice."

"Those are very thin definitions, my dear. Can you try a little harder?"

Her "my dears" are beginning to irritate me. At first they seemed friendly and sincere but now they sounds patronizing.

"I don't know. Things that are aesthetically pleasing?" I look at her for approval, but she doesn't appear impressed. I think back to high school art class and use all the big words I can recall. "Perfectly symmetrical? Contrasting objects or colours in a harmonious juxtaposition?"

She shuts me down with a brief, but strong: "Beauty, my dear, is exception."

She allows me a moment to absorb her statement before she confidently continues.

"A thing of beauty is a thing that stands out to us. Beauty grips to our memories and beauty moves us to action. And it is always undeniably and completely authentic because the beauty in the eye and heart of the beholder can never be forged. So, with this definition, what is more beautiful than pain and suffering?"

"I understand. You're saying pain and suffering is a unique part of us."

"I am saying it may be the only part of us that is authentically us. We are taught the things that will supposedly make us happy—money, love, smarts, looks, popularity, and so on—and we chase them in our youth, like well-trained horses at a race. But our pain is our own, like a secret chamber behind our vibrant self-portraits, and what each one of us does with it is what defines and differentiates us."

Amatullah's words force a bleak slideshow of my life in my mind. I think about the caricature in my mind that represents me before this unique year, before meeting the Red One. She didn't do much but hide away from the world. She even created a whole different persona to avoid herself. When she couldn't find the energy to continue pretending, she found the Red Powder. She was and is, indeed, just a drug addict. The drug is her agency.

"Sometimes you can't do anything with it." I speak as confidently as Amatullah now. "Your pain runs your life. It does you. It becomes you."

"No, my dear, we all do something with it. Refusing to acknowledge pain and choosing to avoid it are both actions that require effort. Many use complete silence to pretend their pain is not there. Many channel it into paintings and poetry and other art and many—" she pauses to turn to me, "—many seek revenge."

A chill runs through my spine. I wonder what she knows and I'm too paranoid to speak now, but every second of silence makes me look guiltier and guiltier.

I force the attention away from me and accuse her instead. "Well, you clearly sought revenge. How does it define you now?"

"Excuse me?"

"I know a few things about your biography. I read a lot about you on the Internet but couldn't find a single article about how you left the slums."

"I ran away in the morning. I ran as fast as I could with no shoes on. We all learn to walk barefoot anyways."

"No, that doesn't make any sense. Abused children don't run." I pause and think about myself almost two decades ago, alone in my room, berating myself in the comfort of familiarity. "Their courage and self-esteem is stolen. They stay put and try to make sense of the abuse, to justify it."

Amatullah slouches slightly. "I do not like to talk about the past too much."

"You killed your pimp, revelled in the glory of payback, but then ran away in fear, didn't you?"

Amatullah quietly looks at her lap.

"You hurt him, didn't you?"

"I did not."

"I know you hurt somebody. That's why your past is so conveniently buried. You chose anger and revenge, and those things don't match your compassionate, humanitarian, yoga-and-chai brand."

Amatullah smiles to herself. I recognize that smile, a smile that is completely out of place and tries its hardest to portray calm. That's the smile I always use to cool down the hot feelings brewing inside.

She interlocks her hands and cracks her fingers rather coarsely. "Nisha, should your ears be the first to hear my deepest secret?"

Amatullah chuckles as she dares me, "How about I tell you my deepest secret in exchange for yours? Then we will truly know each other."

My deepest secret is gasping for breath behind us in the trunk of the car. My deepest secret if revealed will land me in jail. But my deepest secret is also so absurd, so improbable, Amatullah won't even believe it.

"Sure." I accept her proposal.

She takes a deep breath and begins, "I may have ended some-body's life, but it was not the life of the animal who sold me. There was a woman whose job it was to take care of me. She was to keep me safe from the men and diseases. She failed."

"Who was she? Did you know her well?"

"Yes, we were as close as a little, obedient girl and an author-itarian woman could be."

My mind makes a deduction I'd rather not confront. I say nothing.

"You are thinking I killed my own mother, Nisha?"

"Did you?"

"She was already dead. The drugs had killed her soul; she was nothing but a pair of skeletal legs walking to get her next fix. She did not take care of me. She made me see men who were known to be violent. She taught me nothing about safety or cleanliness. She would kiss me in the mornings, as if her kisses would somehow put out the hellfire of the previous night."

"I'm sorry."

"I was young and impulsive, and I could not hold the ball of pain and rage in my hands too long. I had to act. I wanted revenge. I wanted my pain to stop."

"What did you do?"

"She overdosed one morning and instead of calling our pimp like I had done the other one hundred times, I stole the money under her mattress and I ran. I ran fast with no shoes on. I still remember the glass and stones cutting my feet."

"So, you didn't take your revenge after all?"

"I did. My revenge was running away and leaving her there to die. I don't know if she died that day, but I knew she would, sooner or later in that hellhole. You see, it was on that day, when I ran through the predatory streets in the middle of nowhere that the universe promised me success. I knew I would become somebody and I chose to leave her there to rot. I never returned or tried to contact her. Even when I was adopted like a common puppy, I never attempted to plead with my new parents to save her."

"She stole your childhood. She abused you. You absolutely did the right thing."

"The right thing—presuming the definition of the right thing being an action that perfectly aligns with our values and sense of justice—should leave us feeling good, should it not, Nisha?"

"Yes."

"Well, I have not felt good for over fifty years now. My act of revenge has burdened me just as much and just as long as my pain. By taking revenge, I became the perpetrator and lost all my power."

"No, you gained power." I disagree so passionately that I can't control raising my voice. "You were powerless before, when she exploited you, and you gave her exactly what she deserved!"

Amatullah is annoyingly calm and emotionless. "My dear, it is the victim who has all the power."

"No!" I say angrily as I speed down the road. "You are wrong." I think about my life as a victim: a dull and repetitive existence shackled to Azar who barely acknowledges me as a thinking and feeling human being. And before him, years and years of my youth spent hiding away, crippled by suffocating memories.

"I don't know how you sold all those books with your completely wrong beliefs."

"Listen to me, Nisha. There are forces in this world. Cool your head and open your ears wide and I will tell you about them." Amatullah places a hand lightly on my shoulder. She doesn't continue to speak until I slow down my driving.

I've stopped shaking. Somehow I'm not afraid of being caught with Sonia's body in my trunk.

"Tell me, what forces?"

"Well, my friends in academia hate to use the words *good* and *evil* so I'll use *love* and *hate* instead. I don't know where these forces came from and I do not know why they persist, but I do know they are both their own catalysts. Acts of love create love within you and so your hands continue to do your heart's work. Acts of hate create hate. One can be filled with blinding hatred and be completely submerged inside that dark force."

"Yes. It's always there," I admit quietly to her. "Even when the day is great and you think you might just be able to move on, it's there."

Amatullah nods and continues, "Perpetrators, most likely victims once upon a time, have chosen to give in to that dark force, creating more and more of it within themselves until they are forever locked up in their lightless cages. Victims still have a choice to stay illuminated—even with the harm of those hateful deeds constantly trying to pull away their souls—you have a choice. Choice is power. Choice is strength. Can the strong, abundant with choice, ever truly be victims?"

Her words overwhelm me. I try to blink away the tears, but I can't stop them from flowing down my cheeks. I can't stop the truth from unfolding in my mind like a blooming flower in the clear, bright sunlight. Amatullah is right, I think. I gave up my choices—it was never I who designed my life. I allowed the evil and hate of others to create this lonely, angry murderer. I am a murderer.

"Why are you crying, my dear?"

Amatullah asking me why I'm crying, seeing the tears I haven't even been able to see myself for half my life, makes me cry even more. I want to tell her everything. I want to confess. I want somebody—another thinking and feeling human being—to hear my pain.

"There's—" I nearly choke as I sob, "—there's a woman in my trunk."

Amatullah puts a comforting hand on my shoulder and nods, "Yes, there's a hidden woman in all of our trunks. To find happiness, we must let her out."

"No, there's an actual woman in my trunk." I force Amatullah's eyes to meet mine. "I might have killed her."

Amatullah moves her hand away from me swiftly and exhales. She begins to look over her shoulder, towards the back of the car, but then changes her mind. "What happened?"

I feel as light as a feather. I don't care anymore about image, reputation, manners, expectations, tomorrow, next week, freedom, or jail. I just want somebody to hear me.

"I met a man. The most attractive man I've ever seen," I confess. "He never told me his name, but I call him the Red One. He made me feel something I've never felt before. Courage? Anger? Rebellious desire? Whatever it was, I knew after I met him that I had to confront my past. I had to confront my life: the relationships in it, the feelings I harbour in myself every day."

"Who was this man?"

"I don't know. I'm really not sure. Maybe a demon or an angel or just a figment of my imagination . . . "

I look to see Amatullah's reaction, but she is serious and attentive. "I don't know if I'll ever see him again, but they say you meet everyone for a reason and no matter who he was, his reason to be a tourist in my life has changed everything. He told me to kill this woman."

Amatullah raises her brows with astonishment, "He told you to commit murder?"

"No, not directly. He planted the thoughts in me. He guided me." I shake my head. "I don't think his intentions were bad. I think he wanted to help me." I point to the back of the car, "Now this woman is pure evil."

"Who is she?"

"She is the reason I can't stand my life. She is the reason I can't be happy. She is the reason I can't connect to anybody. I can't love anybody. I can't love me. I can't stand up for myself. I can't speak what I feel. I can barely feel. I can't do what I want. I can't—"

"Then you did the right thing killing her, Nisha."

"What?"

"You did the right thing." Amatullah looks at me reassuringly. "I will help you get rid of her for good."

I chuckle at her bluff and insist, "You can call the police if you want to. It's fine. I've accepted that my life as I knew it is gone. I'm ready to face the consequences."

"You will not have to face anything if there is no proof, my dear." Amatullah removes her purse from her lap and rests it to her side, assuring me that she isn't reaching for her cellphone. "It is dark now and all the joggers and children must have gone home. Stop by the first park you see and let us have a look in the trunk."

"Are you sure you want to see her?"

"Well, we cannot take her to the gala, can we?"

"She might still be alive."

"Then we must kill her before we get rid of her."

I look at Amatullah with disbelief but see no sign of deception.

"You can trust me. Now go." Amatullah looks at the map on my phone and forces me to make a U-turn. "There is a ravine right behind us."

I feel like I'm lost in a strange dream as I mindlessly turn the car, preparing to get rid of a dead body with the assistance of an international celebrity under a moonlit sky in the middle of nowhere. I don't know who I am anymore. I can't recognize the eyes in the rear-view mirror. I can't recognize the hands on the steering wheel.

I turn into the park with my heart pounding in my cold chest. I'm so numb I can hardly control the pressure of my foot on the pedal. I speed down the driveway to the parking lot at a dangerous pace.

"Slow down," Amatullah warns, "you might kill a deer."

I wonder at the irony of her concern.

I swerve into a tiny gravel parking lot and stop the car abruptly. Amatullah and I both jerk from the impact. We undo our seatbelts and get out of the car onto the gravel. We are surrounded by dark silhouettes of the trees; in the distance, the dim, eerie glow of streetlights; up above, the stars and the moon. I hear crickets and a shuffling among the leaves. I hear my heart beating violently inside me.

"Are you ready?" Amatullah speaks over the deafening heartbeat.

"I don't know."

"We are very late to this gala and if we do not hurry up now, I will miss the slot for my speech. That will appear incredibly rude and we do not want that."

She turns to me, puts a hand on my arm, and asks softly, "Nisha, were you abused as a child?"

I nod and try to say yes but no word escapes my dry mouth.

"Sweetheart," Amatullah looks up at the sky and back at me. "Were you sexually abused?"

"Yes. I was twelve."

"This woman in the trunk is the perpetrator?"

"No. Her brother."

"So why is she paying for the sins of her brother?"

"He's dead," I sob, "and she knew all about it and she didn't stop it. She encouraged it. She led me to him."

"I see." Amatullah takes a deep breath of the night air. "Stop crying now, dear, and open the trunk quickly."

We go to the back of the car and I open the trunk.

I see Amatullah standing fearlessly over the slightly open trunk door. With her hands on her hips, she waits impatiently for me to open it. Finally, in the silence of the deserted park, I hear Sonia's faint mumbles.

Amatullah, to my surprise, does not acknowledge Sonia's cries. She says, in a cold and crisp loud voice, "You should have a heavy rock ready."

For a moment, I foolishly don't understand what I would need a rock for. I stop in my tracks when I realize what Amatullah is advising me to do. She motions with her hand for me to hurry. I look around and there is no shortage of rocks at the edges of the parking lot. With shaking legs and aching feet in heels, I stumble across the gravel. I move further away from the car and the increasingly desperate muffled cries of Sonia as I search for a rock in the dark. I find one the size of a cantaloupe and as I drag it up with my sweaty hands, I let out a grunt. This is my war cry.

"Put it down and help me get her out of the trunk," Amatullah instructs. "You must do it away from the car unless you want to clean blood all night."

I am stunned by the absolute coldness of the refined woman before me—this woman who is famous for preaching about compassion and sympathy. Her indifference is helping me commit my crime. She is condoning it. I put the rock down and stand beside her, to draw in some of her icy energy. Then I hold

214 SAFIA FAZLUL

the edge of the trunk door and brace myself to see Sonia one last time.

Sonia lies there in her bra and panties tied up with the ropes and the duct tape exactly as I had left her. I can see, under the clear moonlight and with no drug tainting my blood, that her cuts and bruises are real. Somebody really did do this to her. Somebody really hurt Aunty Khan's daughter. I did it.

Sonia's large and bloodshot eyes are no longer angry or brave; they are frightened and desperate as she continues mumbling behind the duct tape without any pause. Before I can unmute her to hear her final words, Amatullah grabs her legs and urges me to grab her upper body.

"Place her on her knees," Amatullah orders as we drop her weak body onto the gravel like a heavy sack.

The rock rests beside me as Sonia kneels before me, weeping and shaking with fear. There is no turning back now.

"Here we are." Amatullah stands behind me with a firm hand on my shoulder. "We live through thousands of days and yet only a few dozen remain in our memories and only a handful take the helm of our lives. Today is one of those days, my dear—which way will it steer?"

I know I must pick up the rock now. I look beyond Sonia's frightened eyes, begging for her life, and remember the justice I was never given. Nothing will ever be done for the pain I've lived through for nearly two decades. Nothing can ever bring back the innocence that was stolen from my childhood. I repeat these truths in my head, adding fuel to my burning rage, but my rationalizing thoughts are interrupted by Sonia's constant moaning.

"Do it then!" Amatullah encourages me.

"Let me hear what she wants to say." I rip off the duct tape from her mouth—and regret it immediately.

I've betrayed myself by allowing her a chance to have her voice. Nobody heard me. I pick up the rock quickly to appease myself, summoning all my strength, rage, and fearlessness to do the inevitable.

Sonia inhales and exhales deeply between her sobs as if she knows this is her last time enjoying the fresh air. Her eyes move from the rock in my hands to Amatullah and finally to me as she forces herself to calm down so she can speak.

"I-I'm sorry, Nisha!" her words are hardly intelligible between all her whimpering. "He touched me too!"

"What?" I step back, the rock in my hands.

"He touched me too," Sonia cries clearly now. "I was just a little girl. I thought he was playing around, but his touches got more and more inappropriate."

"Is she lying?" Amatullah mutters into my ear as if I would know the answer.

"I'm not lying," Sonia can't bear to look me in the eyes anymore. "I told my mother. She did nothing. She didn't even believe me. She told me to shut up for my own good."

Sonia's chillingly familiar scenario leaves me weak. The rock drops from my hand.

"Why?" I shriek and grab her chin to force her to look me in the eyes. "You knew what he was. Why did you send me to his room?"

"You weren't the only one . . . I thought if I could turn his attention to other girls, he'd leave me alone."

"You could've told somebody right then or years later. A teacher? A cop? A neighbour?"

"He was my brother and I loved him. I didn't want him to get into trouble."

"That is not an adequate explanation," Amatullah tells me. "You better pick up that rock again—"

"—And I was angry." Sonia goes on. "I was mad at him, myself, my mother, the entire fucking world. He destroyed my childhood and somebody else should also feel my pain."

I bury my face in my hands. I sob like a child—that same child that was sitting in her room eighteen years ago beside a mother who wouldn't help her—as Amatullah's gentle but protective hand pats my back.

"I'm so sorry, Nisha," Sonia says softly, "my life was also destroyed. It might look like my life is perfect, but I've been in and out of rehab the past twenty years. You are not the only one who has suffered."

Amatullah turns and looks at Sonia but speaks to me about her instead, "Here is a wretched one who appears to have rejected love and given in completely to hatred. You've both walked the path of darkness all this time, but are you going to join her in its eternal cage tonight?"

"No." I stop crying and step away from Sonia. "We're the same, her and I, but I refuse to be her."

Amatullah smiles at me with pride and approval. "You are no longer a victim, my dear." She begins to lead us towards the car, not paying any attention to Sonia's protests.

"You can't just leave me here!" Sonia falls over into the gravel as her breasts spring out of her bra. "Help! Somebody help me!"

"What are we going to do with her?" I beg Amatullah for a solution as I fix Sonia's bra, covering her nudity.

"I will make a phone call. Somebody will be here shortly to clean her up and take her home."

"Who's going to do that?"

"It is not hard to find somebody in Toronto willing to do good."

19

ALL EYES ARE on me. That's what I wanted anyway. My curls are in every direction, my makeup has melted down my face, my saree is dripping beads and dragging on the floor behind me like a badly wrapped bedsheet. I left my heels in the car because they hurt my soles and now my dirty, bare feet poke out from behind the frayed saree with every step.

I walk into the foyer with the tall ceilings and grand chandeliers, like a bomb amongst the beautiful people in their dazzling jewellery and silk ties. I walk slowly towards the crowds, like an accidental drop of paint dripping onto a perfect canvas. They all stop chatting about their next exotic vacation for a second to stare at me in awe.

The whispers and chuckles begin and not a single person in the lobby asks if I'm all right. I remove the edge of my saree off my shoulder, wrap it around my hips, and scandalously expose my stomach and cleavage. I want to give them something more to talk about.

"Nisha, what happened?" A familiar voice asks in my ear.

I turn around to find Mariam in a bedazzled hijab, looking almost unrecognizable with her heavy makeup. Her cellphone is in her hand, of course.

"I'm great." I tell her with a genuinely confident smile. "I'm not staying long so if you want a selfie with me, take it now."

Mariam hesitates to find her next words and utters, "Don't you want to fix yourself up first?"

"No." I smile. "Like I said—I'm not staying long."

Mariam takes our picture quickly. She looks frightened and I look like a happy raccoon with all the black mascara and eyeliner around my eyes. This should get Mariam's social media page a lot of views and make her the centre of attention for a few hours.

I don't have to be here. I could be at home, comfortable in my pajamas, eating ice cream and watching mind-numbing TV shows. I could be in my room, reading one of Amatullah's books, and planning my future. That's what I want to do—plan a future as long and as bright as I can imagine; one that keeps me smiling if I'm lucky enough to reach a hundred years. But I have unfinished business.

I enter the hall where the massive number of people and the darkness and moving purple spotlights take the attention away from me. The main stage where Amatullah will deliver her speech is decorated with large posters of brown-skinned girls, clearly impoverished with rotting teeth and ripped clothes. I don't understand the point of putting up those posters. I wonder if any of those girls—real human beings who may or may not be alive right now—have agreed to be the face of charity or the object of the wealthy West's guilt.

There must be a thousand people here, sitting at their tables or walking around networking. I always felt completely insignificant in a gathering this large. I felt unimportant and phony, just another mortal fish in a sparkling pond swimming along with the others. But tonight, I see the individuals in the crowd.

These are not just one thousand mortals; these are one thousand irreplaceable stories, thoughts, dreams, sins, and good deeds. And among them, I too am irreplaceable, deserving of distinction.

I find the table we were assigned in our tickets. My seat is empty and of course Ikram and Simi's seats are too. I see Azar's profile in the dark, hunched over his phone. My handsome husband is sitting alone, across Tanzila and Rabia and their husbands, and not strutting around like a peacock. He has a familiar frown on his face.

I catch Tanzila's eye and then Rabia's, and they both rise to greet me. They pretend like my appalling cleavage, naked stomach, and dishevelled appearance aren't there. They hug me, put on a big show of friendship for their waving husbands, and then sit down. I'm Azar's problem now.

Azar smiles for the rest of the table and pulls my chair out like a gentleman. He comes closer to me, gritting his teeth with hidden anger.

He whispers furiously into my ear while holding his smile in place, "What the hell happened to you? Go fix your saree!"

I ignore him and instead ask curiously, "Tell me, did you ever send me red lilies?"

"Huh? Did you forget? You sent yourself lilies because it was part of your healing process or some stupid nonsense." Azar's cheeks are red with embarrassment. "Where the hell are your shoes?"

"What about the business card in my purse—with the dentist's name on it? Did you put it there?"

"Why would I put it there? You told me you've been looking for a new dentist—you said you were visiting different offices to find the right one."

"I see."

"Now can you please go fix yourself. You look like you were attacked by a bear!"

"What if I was, Azar?" I turn to him, my eyes locking into his, with no pretend smile or lowered volume. "What if I was mauled by a bear? Would you blame me or the bear?"

I can feel Rabia and Tanzila and their husbands turning their heads to stare at us.

"Stop this stupid act of yours!" Azar grips my thigh violently under the table. "Excuse yourself politely to the washroom right now."

"Will you kill me if I don't?" I raise my voice and Azar releases my leg. "Will you hurt me in front of all these people? What will they say? What will your boss say? What will Linda say?"

"That's what this damn attitude lately is about? Linda?" Azar looks around in all directions, making sure he catches anyone who dares listening in on our conversation.

"Yeah, your mistress." I announce to the table.

"Keep your voice down!" Azar still has the audacity to smile for everybody at our table who's looking our way now with concern.

I raise my voice to make sure everybody sitting here and at the neighbouring tables hears me loud and clear, "Did she keep her voice down when you fucked her?"

Azar cowers in his seat as he continues with a low volume, "Look, she's a young graduate who's just trying to move up the ladder. She is trying to get with me so I can help her, but I have no interest—"

"I saw the texts and pictures, Azar."

Azar backs off and sits back into his chair, refusing to acknowledge the stares of his friends. His fake smile is finally gone. Rabia and Tanzila and their husbands quietly leave the table. They can't bear to watch the collapse of Azar and Nisha, the perfect couple.

I reach under the table and put my hand on his thigh now. Lovingly.

I lean into him and whisper, "We wanted something everybody else had—even though we both always knew it wasn't for us. Not everybody is ready to be paired up just because they've reached a certain age. People are different and so are paths. I forgive you and I hope you can forgive me."

"Forgive you for what?"

The words feel heavy as I try to roll them out. They are tied back by the weight of family, culture, obligation, expectation, fear. But I have the strength now to tell Azar, "I'm leaving you. We are finished. I want a divorce."

Azar's eyes fill with tears. I have never seen his eyes glossy before. The sight fills me with deep sadness because I have finally been given back what I lost as a little girl: compassion. I don't want to hurt anybody.

Azar holds his tears back and returns to whispering in my ear. "I made a mistake. I love you, Nisha."

"No, you love success, Azar. You love being seen as successful. You want a beautiful, never-aging wife and a healthy baby boy so that pretty picture of yourself in your head can evolve. You do not love me. You never loved me."

"Have you lost your mind, Nisha?" Azar speaks in a normal volume now, finally not caring who's watching or listening to us. "Did you see the psychiatrist I told you to see?"

"No, but I saw somebody much more helpful," I say as I turn towards the stage where an announcer begins his introduction for Amatullah.

All conversations come to an abrupt stop, the hall is darkened and a slideshow of Amatullah's life, writings, and charity work commences on the screen behind the announcer. Everybody sits in awe and watches the story of a great woman. But only I know how truly great she is. "You need more of the Red Powder. It's the only thing that can help you," Azar grumbles.

"No more drugs, Azar. No more Red Powder. No more red anything."

The memories of the Red One flash through my mind; the naked moments of feeling alive and not being watched by any pair of eyes, the pleasure I may or may not ever experience again. They are good memories and mine to keep no matter what the future holds.

"Only I can make myself feel better. I want to get better."

The slideshow ends and the announcer finishes his presentation. A spotlight shines on the guest of the evening as she emerges on the stage, smiling and waving. Everybody in the room, except Azar and I at our empty table, stand up with applause.

Azar's sad face reverts into a cold, hate-filled visage as he laughs at me, "You're going to get better all by yourself? You can't make anything happen. You don't have a dollar to your name. You have nothing without me. Where will you go?"

"I'll accept your help if you will give it to me." I kiss his cheek and stand up to leave. "If not, I'll run. I'll run away in the morning with no shoes on."

Behind me, Amatullah clears her throat and begins her speech.